She was never to be trusted, yet the thought of her in his brother's arms had enraged him

Except, now she was in his arms. Now she was his.

He should leave now while he could. He shouldn't take her when his emotions were this wild and troubled.

And perhaps he would have left if that tiny sound of need hadn't escaped her parted lips. If her fingers hadn't uncurled from those tight fists and splayed on his chest.

One strap had slid down her arm, and he could see that her skin was as smooth as cream. At that moment, she looked like a Grecian goddess come to life. Diana perhaps. Or Persephone.

Or Venus?

Reasoning went up in flames.

All about the author...
Janette Kenny

For as long as **JANETTE KENNY** can remember, plots and characters have taken up residence in her head. Her parents, both voracious readers, read her the classics when she was a child. That gave birth to her deep love for literature and allowed her to travel to exotic locales—those found between the covers of books. Janette's artist mother encouraged her yen to write. As an adolescent she began creating cartoons featuring her dad as the hero, with plots that focused on the misadventures on their family farm, and she stuffed them in the nightly newspaper for him to find. To her frustration, her sketches paled in comparison with her captions.

Her first real writing began with fan fiction, taking favorite TV shows and writing episodes and endings she loved—happily-ever-afters, of course. In her junior year of high school, she told her literature teacher she intended to write for a living one day. His advice? Pursue the dream, but don't quit the day job.

Though she dabbled with articles, she didn't fully embrace her dream to write novels until years later when she was a busy cosmetologist making a name for herself in her own salon. That was when she decided to write the type of stories she'd been reading—romances.

Once the writing bug bit, an incurable passion consumed her to create stories and people them. Still, it was seven more years and that many novels before she saw her first historical romance published. Now that she's also writing contemporary romances for Harlequin, she finally knows that a full-time career in writing is closer to reality.

Janette shares her home and free time with a chow-shepherd mix pup she rescued from the pound, who aspires to be a lapdog. She invites you to visit her Web site at www.jankenny.com. She loves to hear from readers—e-mail her at janette@jankenny.com.

Janette Kenny
CAPTURED AND CROWNED

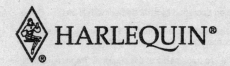

TORONTO • NEW YORK • LONDON
AMSTERDAM • PARIS • SYDNEY • HAMBURG
STOCKHOLM • ATHENS • TOKYO • MILAN • MADRID
PRAGUE • WARSAW • BUDAPEST • AUCKLAND

Recycling programs
for this product may
not exist in your area.

ISBN-13: 978-0-373-12962-1

CAPTURED AND CROWNED

First North American Publication 2010.

www.eHarlequin.com

Printed in U.S.A.

CAPTURED AND CROWNED

PROLOGUE

"I DON'T want to marry the Crown Prince, Papa."

It had taken Demetria Andreou two days to work up the courage to say that to her father. She'd waited until Sandros Andreou was relaxing by the pool by the palace guesthouse, with plates of *meze* and a bottle of ouzo before him. She'd waited until she was sure there was no hope that the relationship would miraculously change between her and her fiancé.

Now, as she watched the olive tinge of her father's skin take on an ugly ruddy hue, she knew his anger was about to explode. And her insides seized up—for his rage was a terrible thing to witness.

"I care little about what you want," her father said. "The King of Angyra selected you to be the Crown Prince's wife when you were twelve years old. It's an honor! A duty to your family and your country!"

It was also a boon to Sandros Andreou, for being the father of the Queen would elevate his status.

"But I don't love him, and he certainly doesn't hold me in any affection."

"Love!" Her father spat the word out as if it were a curse. "Foolish girl! By the time you are twenty-three years old you'll be the Queen of your own kingdom. Young, rich beyond measure, and never having to want for anything."

Anything but love. Anything but the freedom to do what she wished to do with her life. Like her dream to design clothes. But her father wouldn't understand that.

Neither had Crown Prince Gregor, when she'd broached the subject to him last night over their annual night on the town, which was meant to show him and his young fiancée having fun. A façade—a pretense of what a normal affianced couple in love would do.

He had merely shrugged and said she was free to pursue it now, but after they were married such a career would be frowned upon. However, he would consider her request to embark on it as a hobby when the time came for such decisions.

She'd known then that arguing the finer points would be useless. She knew that her life as Queen would be lonely. Cold. Miserable.

Surely she wasn't the only woman who'd be suitable as the Queen of Angyra! Surely the Crown Prince could find favor with another woman.

"Perhaps if you spoke with the King this evening he'd reconsider..."

"No! That is out of the question," her father said, the underlying threat in his voice chilling her to the bone. "You will marry Crown Prince Gregor Stanrakis one year from today, as your King demands. Is that clear?"

"Yes, Father."

But moments later her heart ached for what would be her very brief career as she took the well-tended path from the palace guesthouse to the equally private beach.

The austere King and her domineering papa had planned her future for her. At least she had a year to make a name for herself in the design world, to follow her dream if only briefly.

For ten years Sandros Andreou had brought his family to

the island kingdom of Angyra as guests of the Royal House of Stanrakis. It was an enchanted place, where the sea sparkled like blue topaz against white sand beaches.

Frangipani and bougainvillea bloomed in profusion, perfuming the air with their sweet spice. Lush stands of olive and cypress covered the rugged mountains that rose majestically against a cloudless sky.

This was old world. Life moved at a slower pace here. The people openly adored their King and Queen. Already they regarded Demetria with open affection.

Her future had loomed as a fairy tale to her when she was young, with the paparazzi snapping photos of her and the handsome Crown Prince on their yearly "date." But now she knew better.

Crown Prince Gregor had only given her a sad smile when she'd brought her worries up to him. "Royalty must marry for duty, not love. That is the way it has always been. I'll be kind to you. All I demand in return is your fidelity until you have given me heirs."

The fact that he still treated her like a child hurt, but not nearly as badly as the cold fate that awaited her. She was to be the virgin bride to a man who didn't even desire her.

Lost in that troubled thought, she left the pristine private beach for the wild lands bordering the royal palace. She walked until the sounds coming from the bustling seaport faded into obscurity. She walked until the palace was no more than a speck in the distance, until the only sound was the wild crash of waves against the rocky shore.

On a slim, deserted stretch of beach littered with driftwood and seaweed she crawled onto a jutting slab of rock and stared out to sea. Life was not fair!

She'd known the Crown Prince for a decade but he was still a stranger to her. After this last visit she held little hope that she'd ever become close with her future husband.

Gregor, ten years older than she, was stoic in the extreme. She'd yet to enjoy her time alone with him. They had nothing in common, which made for very stilted conversations. He'd never even given her more than a perfunctory kiss, and she was sure he'd done that just for show!

There was no romance between them. No passion.

No love.

"What are you doing here?" a man asked, startling her with his closeness.

She shielded her eyes and stared down at the stranger, hoping he wouldn't recognize her. He in turn stared back at her as if he'd never seen her before.

Either a local or a tourist. She decided on the latter, since he was unaware of her identity.

She took a breath and gave the man a closer study. He wore low-slung shorts and sandals, and a knowing smile that took her breath away.

Without a doubt he was the most handsome man she'd ever had the pleasure of meeting. The wind had tousled his wealth of black hair and the sun had turned his tall, muscular body a rich bronze.

And his dark eyes... They glowed with a mesmerizing combination of amusement and desire. All directed at her!

"Well?" he asked when she continued to gape.

"I'm enjoying the view as well as the peace and quiet," she said, and hoped that the turmoil of emotions churning within her weren't written on her face, that he couldn't tell her heart was racing and her insides were tied in knots. "What about you? Why are you here?"

He pointed at the beach, where his footprints remained in the sand. "I've been inspecting the nesting grounds of chelonia mydas. Green sea turtles."

"You're a conservationist?" she asked.

This time his devilish smile was brief. "This beach is closed to locals and tourists. You should leave."

Yes, she should—but not for the reason he cited. This handsome man who embodied the sand and the surf and all things wild was a danger to her senses, for already he was making her feel things she'd only read about. Dreamt of one day having with her husband. And this dark-haired stranger hadn't even touched her, yet alone kissed her!

Kissed her? Heat flooded her face at the wicked thought.

Yes, she should leave. Put as much distance as possible between her and this charismatic man.

Instead she heard herself say, "Tell me more about your work here."

"It is—"

He broke off at the odd sound of thrashing in the water. His gaze jerked toward the sea and he muttered an oath.

Before she could register what had changed his mood, he'd vaulted onto the slab of rock beside her, sitting so close she felt the heat of his powerful length brand her, so close each breath she managed to drag in brought his unique scent of the wild sea deep into her lungs.

"No," she said when he wrapped an arm around her waist and yanked her against him. "Let me go!"

But the last words almost never left her, because he'd clamped his hand over her mouth. Her pulse raced like the wind, for she was no match for the steely strength she felt in him.

Helpless in a man's hold again.

Before full-blown panic overtook her, he whispered in her ear, "Don't make a sound or you'll startle them."

She tore her gaze from his intense one and looked to the sea. Emerging from the surf were lumbering sea turtles, all moving in a mass up the beach as if they were certain of their destination.

They were simply magnificent to watch. The tension gripping her eased and she relaxed against his warm, muscular chest, awed to see this slice of nature up close. Hands that had pushed against him slipped around his torso now, holding him tight as he held her.

And that was how they stayed for an hour or more, arms entwined and bodies pressed together. Two people lucky enough to witness an amazing tableau.

When the last turtle had laid her eggs and returned to the sea, she looked up at the man she clung to and smiled. "That was the most fascinating thing I've ever seen."

He flashed his devilish smile and stroked his fingers along her cheek, the feather-like touch sending ripples of sensual awareness crashing through her. "I've never enjoyed it more than at this moment, *agapi mou*. You made this special."

The endearment melted her heart, but the passion kindled from his nearness left her trembling for more. This was new. Powerful. Addictive.

A part of her brain registered that what she was feeling and wanting was wrong, that being here in this handsome stranger's arms could only lead to heartache.

But she couldn't find the strength to pull away.

Her body naturally bowed into his, her face lifting in silent entreaty. "I hate for it to end."

"It doesn't have to."

If she'd had a protest it was silenced when his mouth swooped down onto hers, commanding, and brimming with all the desire her lonely heart ached for. She clung to him as he pushed her back onto the rock, soon lost in drinking from his kisses like one delirious with thirst.

The rock was hard and hot beneath her, but so was the earthy man stretched out beside her. Without breaking the kiss, she was barely aware of his hand sliding under her T-shirt, of the electrifying sensations of his bare skin brushing hers.

His big hand cupping her bared breast thrilled and shocked her. A sliver of sanity prevailed. "No—"

"Yes," he said, thumbing one nipple into such a hard peak that she squirmed and moaned.

Resistance was laughable when all she wanted was more of his touch, his kiss. And he granted her that wish by shoving her shirt out of the way and capturing her breast in his mouth.

He suckled hard. New sensations exploded within her and her back arched off the rock. Her fingers tangled in his hair, holding him close, as she reveled in her very first taste of passion.

She couldn't imagine voicing a protest when his hand slipped inside her shorts to fondle that very private part of her. No man had ever touched her so, and though she'd read of it the reality was far more erotic.

And when he slipped his fingers inside her thoughts simply ceased as a new and powerful need consumed her. She closed her eyes and clutched at him as she was carried up toward the sun on a tight spiral.

A rainbow of lights exploded behind her eyes. Bells sang out, just as she'd always imagined it would be at this moment.

Bells?

No! Those weren't the bells of passion she heard but the tolling of the village church bells. Five times. In one hour she had to present herself at the royal palace for dinner with the royal family.

She should be fussing over what to wear instead of frolicking on the beach with a stranger. Instead of granting him this intimacy that should be reserved for her husband. How could she have let this happen?

She shoved away from her pagan god from the sea, shaken by the desire still swirling within her like a whirlpool, threatening to drag her back into the languid depths of passion once more if she let it.

"Stop it," she said, and frantically righted her clothes with fingers that felt awkward.

"As the lady wishes," he said, the beautifully chiseled lips that had adorned her body now pulled into a wry smile.

She shook her head, ashamed at what she'd done. Shamed that her body still yearned for more of the same.

Without another word she scrambled off the rock and ran. But even when she was back in the guesthouse, in her room, she realized that she'd never forget this stolen moment with a stranger.

Prince Kristo Stanrakis strode into his father's royal office, wishing he were anywhere but here. Though he loved his homeland, his passions rested elsewhere.

Then too he didn't look forward to being present for this dinner tonight, with the Andreou family. After that first one ten years ago, where the King had announced that Gregor was to marry Andreou's daughter, with the too-big eyes and rail-like form, he'd managed to miss every visit. Until now.

This was a royal decree and nobody, not even a grown prince, could ignore it. Not without incurring the King's wrath.

He strode straight to the King and went down on a knee. "You look well, Your Majesty."

His father snorted. "How good of you to tear yourself away from the gaming tables."

"My duties as ambassador can be taxing," he said—a joke, for if that was all he did with his time he'd be bored out of his mind.

As usual, his father scowled at the offhand remark. For years the King had found disfavor with Kristo for his errant ways, expecting him to spend more time on Angyra. Anything that took time away from official duties was inconsequential to the King, so Kristo had ceased bringing the subject up anymore.

"Rest assured I will be present when the State Council convenes next week," Kristo said, and earned a wave of dismissal from the King.

They both knew he'd leave Angyra as soon as that duty was satisfied. Or perhaps not this time, he thought as he crossed to his brothers.

After the interesting diversion he'd had this afternoon on the beach, staying could prove interesting. He'd never met a woman who was as entranced by the wilds of nature as he. He'd never shared that kind of moment with anyone before.

That fact had made the explosive passion all the more sweet. Even now his body stirred at the memory of holding such perfection in his arms.

If the church bells hadn't tolled, there was no telling how far she would have let him go.

"About time you showed up," Gregor said.

Kristo took the glass of *tsipouro* the server handed him and took a sip before answering the Crown Prince. "The sea turtles were nesting, so I couldn't leave until they did. Where is your fiancée?"

"She just arrived," Gregor said, and yet no sign of elation or pleasure showed on his features. "If you'll excuse me?"

Kristo smiled at his other brother. "He is just like Father—far too intense."

"He'll be a good king," his younger brother Mikhael said. "The question is will he be a good husband to his young Queen?"

Kristo imagined that Gregor would follow in their father's footsteps there as well. His marriage hadn't been a love match, and he doubted the Crown Prince's was either.

"Your Majesty," Gregor said, his voice ringing with

authority. "I present my betrothed—Demetria, the future Queen of Angyra."

Kristo turned, and the welcoming smile on his face froze. No! It couldn't be her!

But it was.

The beautiful woman his brother was escorting toward them was the same one he'd kissed to distraction an hour ago!

No, not just kissed.

The delicate stem of his wineglass popped in his tight grip, and his blood roared angrily through his veins.

Just an hour ago he'd tasted Demetria's full, sensual lips. He'd held the weight of her lush breasts in his hands, known the silken texture of the skin, the tight budding of her nipples.

Gregor, unaware of the fury building within Kristo, escorted his fiancée toward him. Her polite smile vanished the moment their gazes locked. Her soft lips parted. Her face drained of color.

"Demetria, this is my brother, Prince Kristo," Gregor said. "I doubt you remember him, since it's been some time since you've seen him."

An hour ago, Kristo thought morosely. One damned hour ago, when he'd brought her to a shuddering climax.

Yet how could he tell his brother that the woman he was to marry was unfaithful? He was just as much to blame for not recognizing her.

"Your Highness," she said, and dipped into a deep curtsy that felt like a mockery in the face of what had transpired between them.

"My pleasure, Demetria," he said, hating the coil he was caught in with her.

She forced a smile and mumbled an appropriate greeting.

In that moment he knew she'd not confess her sin either. And why should she?

Wealth and position awaited her.

Damn her for her perfidy! He hated her more than he did anyone on earth.

After today, he vowed to avoid the royal palace *and* his brother's unfaithful fiancée.

CHAPTER ONE

'RINCE KRISTO STANRAKIS had never thrown a royal fit of nger in his life, but he was moments away from doing so just ow. He flung his tuxedo jacket on a red brocade Louis XV haise and ripped open his stark white shirt, sending a row of iamond studs flying. One pinged off an inlaid table before alling to the gold Kirman carpet, while another chinked as hit a window.

This urgent meeting with the future King, his lawyers and he highest officials was over. Angyra would face change yet gain.

His life had just been turned on its heel and there wasn't a amned thing he could do to evade his fate.

No! His *duty*!

He paced the impressive length of his apartment. *Duty!* How he hated that word. How he hated *her*!

Just one month ago they'd buried their father, the beloved King of Angyra. *She'd* come to the funeral and sat with her father and sister, looking solemn and royal and aloof. Looking sexy as hell in a black sheath that had hugged her luscious curves.

He hadn't seen her in almost a year, yet the moment their eyes had met he'd been slammed him back to that day on the beach. A roiling mix of guilt, rage and desire had boiled in him.

He wanted nothing to do with her. Yet he still wanted her more than he'd ever wanted a woman.

Being near her needled him with guilt for betraying his brother and he did not like that feeling one bit. But he'd been prepared to suffer through her return in less than two weeks to marry King Gregor. Except that would not happen now!

The rap at his door was preceded by its opening. He whirled to find Mikhael striding into his suite, with a bottle of ouzo under his arm and two glasses clutched in one hand.

"I thought you could use this," Mikhael said, and promptly poured two drinks.

He took the offered liquor and tossed it back, relishing the bite to his senses. "Did you have any idea that Gregor was ill?"

Mikhael shook his head. "He's seemed tired of late, and complained of headaches, but I attributed it to the stress of assuming Father's duties."

The same thought had crossed Kristo's mind. He'd never dreamed that Gregor had secretly seen a doctor just before the King's death, only to discover two days ago that he had inoperable cancer.

The prognosis was grim. With death imminent, Crown Prince Gregor had chosen to abdicate before the State Council proclaimed him King of Angyra tomorrow.

That official announcement had been made just one hour ago.

By order of birth, the crown now passed to Kristo. He was now Crown Prince, which had thrown the council into emergency session. Unless they deemed him truly unfit to rule—which was possible, considering his reputation—the accession ceremony would take place tomorrow promptly at eleven in the morning.

As if that weren't jarring enough, he was now forced to assume his brother's betrothal agreement as well! He had to

marry Demetria Andreou—in less than two weeks, if he kept
to the schedule that had been set in place.

Damn the fates!

Desirable, unfaithful Demetria would be *his* wife. His
Queen.

"I don't look forward to tomorrow."

"For what it's worth, I think you'll be a good King,"
Mikhael said.

Kristo wasn't so sure. Though he'd done his duty to the
State Council, and sat in on required meetings, he'd paid little
heed for he'd been in reality no more than a figurehead.

However, he'd taken his role as ambassador much more
seriously, as that had allowed him to wine and dine dignitaries around the world. Gambling and carousing, as his father
had called it.

At times that had been true. But the setting had allowed him
to do what came naturally. In turn, being away from Angyra
had allowed him the freedom to do what he really wanted.

But that would soon be in the past.

"Has he contacted Andreou yet?" Kristo asked.

"He was speaking with him by phone when I left."

How would Demetria take the change of plans?

Kristo stopped before the palatial window and looked out
on the terraced garden that stepped down to the cerulean sea.
He splayed his hands on the casing so hard that he felt the
heavy moldings imprint on his flesh.

Dammit, he didn't *want* to be King! And by hell's thunder
he certainly didn't want to marry Demetria!

But the only way to surmount his fate was by death or
abandonment of his country. Though he'd joked that he could
walk away from Angyra and never miss it, the truth of the
matter was that he couldn't shirk his duty.

"Gregor felt certain that Andreou wouldn't balk at the

change of plans," Mikhael said. "He suspects that the lady might feel differently."

"How she feels doesn't matter. She has a duty to uphold."

"True, but you are a stranger to her."

In some ways, but in others they were intimately acquainted. But that was his guilty secret to bear.

"As Gregor pointed out today, the betrothal contract simply states that Demetria is to marry the Crown Prince," Kristo said, chafing over the fact that he was now that man. "Surely she is aware of that fact."

"You are being callous about this, brother."

"I'm simply being pragmatic," Kristo said. "Demetria and I are bound by the same laws. There is nothing left to discuss."

The Royal House of Stanrakis had one ancient and non-breakable rule. All future rulers must be of noble Greek blood. As the Stanrakis family continued to produce males, their Crown Princes had only to find a noble bride of Greek blood.

Easier said than done. But then, they weren't marrying for love. Even if such a thing existed, it wasn't ordained for a Stanrakis prince.

It certainly wouldn't be for him!

Demetria had been handpicked by the King. She had been groomed to be the next Queen of Angyra.

She possessed the right lineage. Her maternal grandfather was Greek—one of the old noblemen like Kristo's father. And her mother had married a Greek, even though Sandros Andreou's blood wasn't as pure.

That man had pricked his temper more times than naught over business dealings. As for Demetria—she fired his lust as well as his anger.

"I still think it would be wise for the sake of your marriage if you would take Demetria aside tomorrow and talk to her," Mikhael said. "It would go a long way in allaying her fears."

Kristo stared into his glass, his smile slow to come. "Yes, you're right."

He'd talk to her, all right. He'd let her know that he'd not tolerate her flirtations. That he'd have her watched carefully since he knew she was not to be trusted.

But the following day at the accession ceremony Demetria was embarrassingly absent.

"Please forgive her, Your Majesty," Sandros Andreou implored as he bent in as deep a bow as a man with such a considerable girth could manage. "Demetria went on a shopping jaunt for her wedding trousseau hours before Crown Prince Gregor abdicated. I haven't been able to reach her on her mobile phone to tell her of the news."

"She is alone?"

The old Greek shrugged. "I'm not sure."

"Don't you know where she went?" Kristo asked, furious that the man hadn't kept a closer eye on his daughter. "Couldn't you send a messenger to find her?"

Sandros Andreou's face turned an ugly purple. "I wasn't sure where to send him, Your Majesty. Her sister thought she went to Istanbul, but the maid thought she went to Italy."

"This is intolerable," Kristo growled. She could be anywhere, with anyone. She could even be entertaining some man!

"Rest assured that when she returns I will have her contact—"

Kristo silenced the man with one wave of his hand that looked surprisingly like the dismissing gesture his father had employed. The wave he'd hated.

"I will see to it myself. Considering the turn of events, it would be wise if your daughter stayed here at the palace until the wedding."

"For twelve days?" Then, as if remembering who he was addressing, Sandros quickly demurred. "Of course, Your Majesty."

"You and your family are welcome to avail yourselves of the guesthouse the day before the wedding."

"The day before?" Andreou repeated.

"Yes. That is all."

The old Greek attempted another bow before taking his leave.

Kristo pushed from his chair and stalked to the window, more restless than he recalled being in years. His gaze fixed on the ridge of mountains in the distance.

Graceful cypresses and thickets of olives blanketed the rugged terrain and helped to conceal Angyra's most treasured commodity. Rhoda gold—a pure metal kissed with a rosy blush and prized all over the world.

The ore taken from the Chrysos Mine had made the Stanrakis family rich beyond measure. It had turned this island kingdom into a mecca that now brought tourists here in droves to buy a trinket made of Rhoda gold.

But an equally rare treasure was the sea turtles. Protecting their nesting ground was his personal challenge, and that had evolved into his secretly backing similar programs worldwide. But who would pick up that challenge now?

"What are you going to do?" Mikhael asked.

The answer was simple. At least to him. "Find Demetria and bring her here."

"But the wedding is less than two weeks away. Women have much to do before such an event."

"She can attend to anything that needs be done here." And he could keep a close watch on her that way.

She would not take a stroll along the beach and entertain a stranger the day before *their* wedding!

"What if the lady refuses?"

He cut his brother a knowing look. "I am not giving her a choice."

Mikhael's eyes went wide. "You can't mean to kidnap her?"

"I most certainly do."

In a small shop in Istanbul, Demetria Andreou unwrapped a yard of Egyptian cotton from the bolt, blissfully unaware of the drama taking place on Angyra. She tested the way the soft fabric shot with silver, copper and gold flowed over her arm like a molten waterfall. Her heart raced with excitement, for when cloth seemed this much alive she knew a garment made of it would positively explode with motion.

"How many bolts of this do you have?" she asked.

"Just this one," the Turkish supplier said. "You like?"

She loved the fabric. It fell naturally into folds when bunched, and it felt gloriously sensuous gliding against bare skin.

It was a wonderful find. To know he only had one bolt almost ensured that no other designer would come out with a garment using the exact same cloth.

Originality was further aided by the fact that she preferred buying fabric from lesser-known markets. Fabric defined style. The best designer in the world was nothing without the appropriate cloth. A design didn't pop until the right fabric was paired with the right fashion.

That was when magic happened. That was when she knew she had created something that could eventually compete side by side with the top fashion houses.

"This is perfect," she told the draper, and earned a smile as she handed him the bolt. "I'll take this one."

He laid it atop the others she'd chosen, and scampered off to select another of his high-end specialty fabrics. She ran a finger over the rich fabric, elated with her finds and yet feeling bittersweet that she wouldn't be able to oversee the making of her designs.

How quickly life had changed for her since the King's death.

In two weeks she'd marry Gregor and become Queen. She'd never get the opportunity to stand in the wings while willowy models sashayed down the catwalks in one of her designs.

But she could still select the fabric for her designs. The fashion show in Athens was two weeks away, and her partner would have precious little time to prepare for what was to be their debut into the fashion world.

While Yannis was living their dream in the design world, she'd be marrying King Gregor Stanrakis.

Chills danced over her skin at the thought, and with it came the flood of shame that she'd have to face Kristo again. How could she possibly marry his brother when it was Kristo she lusted for? How could she sit across a table from her husband's brother and not be tormented by memories of him kissing and fondling her on that beach?

The answers continued to elude her as the draper bustled from the back room, bearing more bolts of fabric. She pushed her worries to the back of her mind and focused on the selections before her.

The first two bolts were easy choices, as they were exactly what she'd envisioned for several of the garments she and Yannis intended to make for their debut line. But her heart raced with delight as light played over the cloth on the last bolt. Was it blue? Green? A combination of both, plus it was shot with magenta.

A midnight carnival of color that constantly moved and changed. The warmth of reds and golds twined with blues and silvers to create a marriage of color that commanded attention.

The cloth was beyond rich. It was regal. Royal.

"I am sorry to have picked this one up," the draper said, and made to take it from her. "This has been damaged in transit and is to be destroyed."

Toss out such beauty?

She refused to relinquish the fabric. This would be the perfect cloth for her signature creation. A loose dress. Flowing. Flirty. A dress that would force her husband to notice her.

The fact there was very little of it left undamaged on the bolt only increased its value.

This was her personal find. The perfect dress for her to wear in her new role as Queen. A garment designed by her for her personal use.

"I will take what you have of it."

"But there is only seven meters. Maybe less."

"It's enough—and please wrap it separately." She'd take this one with her for it was her find. Her treasure.

With the last bout of shopping over, she paid her bill with a degree of sadness. When she married, jaunts like this would be unheard-of. She'd have guards around her. She'd have obligations. She'd in essence be a prisoner of her duty.

After securing delivery of the material to Yannis, who was at her flat in Athens, Demetria left the draper's shop with a sense of dread. Freedom as she knew it was quickly ending for her. The next twelve days would certainly fly by too quickly.

Since she'd forgone lunch, and eaten only a piece of fruit for breakfast, she decided to sate her hunger with takeaway food. But even that she'd have to hurry. She dared not miss the ferry back to Greece or her papa would fly into a fury again.

She'd started up the lane when a sleek limo whipped around

her and stopped. Before she could register that it had blocked her way, the doors flew open and two men jumped out.

Both were huge. Both wore menacing frowns. Both came at her.

Her instincts screamed *run*. But before she could force her legs to move a third man emerged from the limo.

Demetria froze as her gaze locked with the one man who'd haunted her dreams.

Prince Kristo of Angyra. His aristocratic features and impressive physique seemed inconsequential under the chill of his cold dark eyes.

"*Kaló apóyevma*, Demetria," he said, but there was no welcoming smile to match the polite form of address. No softening of his chiseled features.

She swallowed hard, unnerved at coming face-to-face with Kristo Stanrakis again. "What is the meaning of this?"

"I am here to escort you to Angyra," he said. "Your marriage to the King will take place in twelve days."

"I'm well aware of when I must marry Gregor, but there is no reason for me to arrive that soon before the wedding."

"Ah, you have not heard the news." His eyes glittered with a startling mix of anger and passion. "Gregor stepped down yesterday."

Had she heard him right? "What?"

"Please—in the car. I do not wish to discuss this further on the street."

As if she had a choice, she thought, as the two large men flanked her. With her stomach now in knots, she moved toward the man she'd kissed to distraction one year ago.

He clasped her elbow, and she jolted as if shocked, for the energy from that touch set her aflame inside. Set her to quivering with a need she'd tried to forget.

She steeled herself against the magnetic pull of him and focused on the startling fact that Gregor was not King. It was too impossible to believe, for surely he'd just taken the crown.

Yet if what Kristo said was true, then why had he said she was to marry the King in less than two weeks?

Just what was going on here?

Knowing she wouldn't get any answers unless she complied, Demetria slid onto the rear seat and scooted to the far side. Kristo climbed in beside her, and despite the roomy interior he simply filled the space with his commanding presence.

"What is this about Gregor stepping down?" she asked.

"Shortly before the King died Gregor discovered that he had a brain tumor," he said, his voice matter-of-fact. "As he didn't wish for Angyra to suffer two Kings dying so close together, or leave a young widow behind, he decided to step down now."

She pressed a hand to her mouth, genuinely stunned to hear he'd fallen victim to such a fate. Her heart ached for Gregor, for though there was no affection between them it pained her to think that his life would be cut short.

"That poor man. I'm deeply grieved to hear this."

"Spare me your false sympathy. We both know you care nothing for my brother. If you did, you never would have offered yourself so freely to a stranger."

She reeled back, as if slapped by the accusation. Denial was pointless, for she *had* succumbed to Kristo. Yet she wouldn't sit here and take his verbal abuse either.

"Yes, I committed a grave error of judgment, and I have regretted my lapse of morals every day since," she said, refusing to cower when his dark brows snapped together over his patrician nose. "But I was powerless to stop the fierce attraction I felt for you."

There. She'd said it at last. But her confession only seemed to anger him more.

Where was the carefree beach bum she'd met that day?

Who was this hard, cold stranger who stared at her with open disgust?

"Are you victim to these fierce attractions often, Demetria?"

"Never before or since."

He snorted and stared out the window. "Of course you'd say that."

As the car smoothly drove on, she stilled the urge to scream in frustration, and asked as calmly as she could manage, "Since you clearly find it so disagreeable to be in my company, why did you come for me?"

"I told you why. I'm escorting you to Angyra."

"This makes no sense," she said. "If Gregor has abdicated, why would I still be required to marry him?"

The beautifully sculpted mouth that had ravished her before pulled into a mockery of a smile. "You won't. The moment my brother rescinded his duty, birth order demanded that I assume the crown and his contractual obligations. I am the King of Angyra. You will marry *me*."

Never! But she bit back that retort. "You can't force me to marry you."

"Ah, but I can, Demetria. I can."

CHAPTER TWO

"THAT'S barbaric," she said.

"It's business. Your betrothal contract states you will marry the Crown Prince of Angyra, or her King if he has already ascended the throne."

She frowned, her face leeching of color, her eyes mirroring her disbelief. Or perhaps it was shock. Perhaps she was as unaware of the exact terms as he'd been.

Not that it mattered. Duty trapped them in this together.

"It's not more specific than that?" she asked, her voice strained now.

He shook his head. "No name is mentioned. You are marrying the title, not the man."

"My God, how cold."

"As I said—it is business."

Though in truth his baser needs were just as demanding as any legality. Just as vexing right now.

It had been a year since Kristo had seen Demetria, and his memory didn't do the lady justice. She was beautiful in a classic sense that called to something deep inside him—something that he refused to acknowledge.

But more troubling was the intense desire that gripped him. Even after a year he could clearly remember the weight of her breasts in his hands, the taste of her skin on his tongue, the sense of triumph that had flooded him when he'd brought her to climax.

And if he allowed himself to admit it there had been a moment of shared tranquility when they'd watched the turtles nesting. He'd never revealed that side of himself to a woman before. He'd never experienced that sense of rightness that had come over him as he'd held her close.

To think he'd done so with a woman who was betraying his brother!

He hated her with the same intensity he desired her, and the combination was wreaking havoc on his senses. How could he marry this woman? How could he ever trust her?

Kristo didn't know, and his fierce attraction only complicated things. He was disgusted with himself for dreaming of the moment when he could claim those full lips again, when he could caress her skin that felt like silk.

Just like the day he'd met her on the beach, her black hair fell loose to her waist in thick curls, free and wild as her soul. Her skin was the palest olive, and looked as if it had never been kissed by the sun.

But it was her eyes that took his breath away. They were dark, yet held a patina that rivaled the finest nuggets of Rhoda gold. And they were wary and assessing him with cool regard.

She hadn't burst into tears when he'd told her of her fate. She hadn't begged him to forgive her or let her go.

No, she'd countered with a strong defiance of her own. And that only made him want her more, for he found her inner strength as attractive as her beauty.

Yet what good did their desire do them? He despised her for betraying his brother, and she hated him for forcing her to honor her betrothal contract. As if he had a choice!

"If the wedding is over a week away, then why must I return to Angyra now?" she asked.

Because he wanted her close by. He wanted to watch her. Touch her. Capture her lips with his and silence her protests for once and for all.

He just caught himself from tossing out that paternal wave that was coming far too naturally. "There is much unrest with the people over the King's death and now Gregor's abdication. They need to see that we are a united front. That they will soon have a King and Queen leading their country again. That Angyra will be stable."

And, as his advisors had suggested, his own status among the people was tarnished from his loose lifestyle. They saw him as the wastrel son. The playboy who chose to party over duty.

As for Demetria—they loved her. She was the fairy princess they'd watched grow up. They'd waited for the day she would become their beautiful young Queen.

They didn't know the truth about her—that she was a beguiling tease. A flirt. Thank God it had been him she'd met on the beach that day!

Just thinking of her doing the same with another man filled him with rage. Had she made a practice of this?

"I assume you've discussed this with my father?" she said at last, sounding resigned. Defeated.

"Yes. He is aware I am bringing you to Angyra," he said.

"He'll join me there, then?"

"No. Your father is invited to the palace the day before the wedding," he said.

Her eyes rounded. "I'll be there alone with you?"

"Come, now. We've already shared an intimacy."

"To my shame," she whispered.

"Was it, Demetria?"

Her lips parted the slightest bit, just as full and inviting as they'd been that day. He wanted her still. In truth his desire for her had not ebbed in the least.

"Now, tell me why I found you in a draper's shop when your father told me you were off shopping for your trousseau."

Her cheeks turned a charming pink—proof he'd caught her in a lie. "If you must know, I was buying cloth for my design partner. The Athens fashion show is in two weeks, and it was to be my debut in the design world."

He stared at her, unsure what to say to that surprising news. "Your father allowed you to hold a job?"

"It's a career. And, yes, my partner and I have designed clothes for the past year and a half."

"Was Gregor aware of this?"

"He was, and he advised me a year ago that it must end when I became Queen."

"But of course. The very idea is ludicrous. The Queen of Angyra would never hold a *job*."

"Career," she countered, in the breath of a whisper. And yet he heard the defiance in that singular word.

That explained why she was in Istanbul shopping for fabric. She was bent on living her life as a designer up until the eleventh hour, when she'd be forced to marry.

"If there is any way we can put the wedding off until after the Athens show—" she said.

"Absolutely not. The marriage must proceed as planned."

The pleasure he'd thought to gain from besting her eluded him. Not that feelings had any place in duty. He was honor-bound to take up the reins his brother had relinquished.

"Your role is to be *my* faithful wife and mother to *my* heirs," he said, putting emphasis on the importance of fidelity while fighting the overwhelming urge to take her in his arms and remind her that they had been very good together one stolen afternoon.

The contradictions she dredged up in him made no sense. He hated this off-balance feeling that gripped him when he was with her, for he didn't know what to do that would make him feel steady again.

At least he wasn't the only one afflicted with uncertainty. He saw her throat work. Saw worry and fear flicker in her eyes.

"You don't love me," she said, shocking the hell out of him with that statement. "You don't even like me."

No, but he desired her more than he'd ever desired a woman. "Our bond is about duty, Demetria. Duty to your family and my country."

"I know that," she said, in a voice heavy with resignation.

She fidgeted with the package she'd bought and bit her lower lip, and he was reminded again of doing the same to her on that sun-kissed slab of rock.

"Would you at least allow me to design my wedding gown? I intended to broach the subject to Gregor at our next visit, but the King's death has set things in motion far too quickly."

"Your gown has already been commissioned," he said. "Gregor obviously saw to it right after the King's demise."

Though Kristo wouldn't have known it if the lavish gown hadn't arrived just before he'd left the palace to fetch her. He'd had it placed in the suite he'd reserved for her. The suite adjoining his own.

It made sense that she get accustomed to her apartments now. To his as well?

The thought had crossed his mind more often than he cared to admit since he'd made the decision to bring her to the palace nearly two weeks before the wedding.

"But I wasn't consulted at all," she said, her voice rising in clear annoyance at his brother's actions.

He was not surprised, for he knew that while women adored lavish gifts of jewels, they could be extremely prickly about choosing their own clothes for special occasions. And nothing could possibly be more special than a royal wedding!

In this regard Gregor was exactly like their father—both experts at orchestrating their lives as well as those around them. Hadn't his brother done much the same with Kristo? Waiting until he'd deemed the time was right to step down from the throne without consulting him? Without alerting him of his duty to claim the crown and the woman?

"Please," she said, and the imploring quaver in her voice drew his gaze back to her. The longing in her beguiling eyes moved him more than he would ever admit, for to do so was weakness on his part. "Allow me this one concession."

Of course one request would lead to another, and another...

He shook his head, thinking it was incomprehensible for the future Queen to make her own clothes, let alone design them. What manner of woman was Demetria? What other secrets was she hiding from him?

"I'll think about it," he said as they reached the airport.

In moments they'd climbed into the tram that would deliver them to his private plane. Again she hesitated before choosing a seat, but his guards decided it for her by placing her between them.

A logical choice to hem her in—so why did he resent being denied her company? He should be glad he was being spared further requests that might pop into her head.

He slammed onto the forward seat beside his chief bodyguard Vasos, vexed with himself for softening toward her. When he was in her company it was far too easy to forget that she'd been unfaithful to Gregor. That given the chance she'd likely betray him as well.

That was what he must bear in mind all the time. She was not to be trusted. Not to be pampered one bit.

He certainly needed to know more about this partner of hers. Needed to know what she'd been doing the past year.

As for bringing Demetria to Angyra? He was asserting his power over her because he could. Because he'd thought of her too much in the past year. Because he wanted her where he could watch her, touch her, kiss her if he so desired.

She was his now. Nothing could stop him from taking her.

Despite her reluctance to return here, Demi thought the island was still breathtaking. A true emerald set amid an azure sea.

But the arrogant man sitting too close beside her was a torment she could live without—especially now, when she struggled to control her emotions around him.

Drawing a decent breath had become a battle, for she pulled his scent deep into her lungs, into her senses. Her skin tingled and an unwanted ache pulsed low in her belly.

As the limo whipped along the serpentine road up the mountain to the palace, she hoped that this time alone together would give them the opportunity to get to know one another on more than an intimate level. Perhaps they'd somehow find a common ground on which to build their future.

Thus far her future revolved around duty to the crown. Marriage. Producing the royal heir as well as other children.

If there was any affection to be had, her life wouldn't loom so grimly. But Kristo didn't even like her. In fact he resented her for surrendering to him one year ago.

There was nothing she could do to change that fact. Nothing.

The drive to the palace was thankfully short. In a frantic effort to put him from her thoughts, she took in the pastoral beauty of the grounds as the car sped up the curved drive. But instead of stopping at the guesthouse, where her family had always stayed during their annual visits, the car continued on toward the house.

"Won't I be given my usual room?" she asked, heart racing more the closer they drew to the massive palace perched on the bluff.

"I've had a suite prepared for you in the palace."

"Why?"

"There is no reason for you to move twice. Besides, it is a matter of security."

Security? No, it was a matter of keeping her under lock and key. Of bending her to his will even before they married.

In the guesthouse she'd have been able to sit by the pool. Enjoy the sauna. Or lounge on the terrace and watch the ships ride the azure sea. She could have taken a walk to the beach and lost herself in thought.

But protesting would get her nowhere. In fact, if she was biddable on this count he might relent on what she really wanted to do. Make her own gown.

So she planted a serene smile on her face as the car stopped on the private terrace at the side of the palace.

Kristo untangled his long legs and got out first, and Demi drew her first decent breath of air. But her reprieve was short-lived.

Though the chauffeur opened the door with a smile, it was Kristo who extended his hand to her. *He* wasn't smiling!

In fact he looked as if he could eat her whole and spit her bones into the sea. Well, in this they agreed. But there was nothing they could do about it.

She swung her legs out the door and laid her hand in his. His fingers closed over hers, sending a rush of nervous energy charging through her. But it was the naked hunger in his eyes as he stared at her bared legs that struck fire to the sensual tinder banked within her.

"Beautiful," he said, his voice a rich rumble of sound as he helped her from the car.

Her body warmed to his. Swayed toward him. She felt the power of the man charge through her, tearing down her resistance just as he had before, on that beach.

And that memory was just what she needed to jerk her hand from his and break the spell. "Thank you," she said, her tone too breathy.

He wanted her because she'd been groomed for this. Because her father had made this arrangement long ago. Because her bloodline was that of the old Greeks who had fought and died for their country.

The palace was as she remembered it from those stiff formal dinners she and her family had endured with the King and Gregor. Jasmine and bougainvillea covered the open-air corridor leading to the door, their mixed scent designed to soothe the senses.

But she was too stressed to appreciate the beauty that greeted her.

She walked down the vast hall paneled in exquisite white marble veined with purple. The cypress floors soon gave way to the thickest Kirman carpet. Chandeliers of glittering crystal hung suspended from twenty-foot-high domes.

Gold ornaments, embellishments and wall escutcheons gleamed a rich rosy hue. But for all its grandeur there was no warmth here.

She remembered that about the palace right away, and wondered if the young princes had ever played here. Had their laughter echoed through the vast chambers? Had they even laughed as children?

Looking at the tall, solemn man walking beside her, she couldn't imagine it. The only time that she recalled any levity here was on the one occasion when she'd met the youngest son, Prince Mikhael.

There certainly hadn't been any humor on her last journey here, when she'd met Kristo. No, only raging passion followed by towering anger when she came to dinner that night and realized the stranger's identity.

At that pregnant moment she'd been sure that he would tell Gregor and her father what they'd done on that beach. She'd almost hoped that he would, for that would surely have broken the betrothal agreement.

She would have been free of this obligation she'd never wanted. But Kristo had never said a word. Neither had she, for she had feared what her father would do to her and her sister if she messed up the opportunity that would surely enrich his life.

Then too she didn't want to follow in her mother's footsteps and be the daughter of scandal. That had only made her last trip more fraught with anxiety.

She'd expected Kristo would tell his brother in private. So why hadn't he? Why had he held their tryst in secret?

Those questions needled her now as he escorted her for what seemed like miles through the palace. Finally Kristo threw open double doors and motioned her inside a room. She stepped into a large suite that was thankfully modern—with the exception of its high ceilings and grand size.

The moment he closed the door and secured their privacy she was very much aware of him as a man. If only he'd smile. If only he'd show more than a glimpse of the man she'd met that day.

Her gaze flicked from his tense expression to the room. The sumptuous sofa and overstuffed chairs lost her interest as she focused on the wedding gown that had clearly been commissioned for her. It was glaringly white, and traditional in the extreme, laden with flounces and heavy beading.

She hated it on first sight. "You can't expect me to wear that hideous gown."

He said nothing for the longest time, but his brow furrowed the longer he stared at it. "It doesn't look that bad to me."

"Then perhaps *you* should wear it."

His lips twitched in the barest of smiles. "I'll stick with a tuxedo."

"I'd prefer that over this," she said.

"Don't think you can sway me with this petulant display."

She heaved a sigh, fists bunched at her sides. "Please, let me sketch the gown I have in mind. You can judge for yourself which one I should wear."

He tipped his head back and stared at her. "You're that sure of your ability to convince me?"

"I'm positive that what I design will be far superior to this stark white monstrosity."

Kristo strode to the gown and fingered the stiff overskirt. "Very well. Make a list of what you need and I will see it is delivered today. But understand that the final decision on what you wear rests with me."

Arrogantly put, and surely not a surprise. The Stanrakis men were noted for their draconian ways.

She walked straight away to the desk, and found paper and a pen. In moments she'd listed the equipment needed: sewing machine, serger, various dressmaker supplies and a dress form.

"I'll need to choose the fabric myself," she said, handing him the list and being careful not to touch him this time.

He eyed her as he might a rare bug on the wall. "You expect me to allow you to go on a shopping jaunt?"

"Yes." She'd been hopeful that her name would have started to be well-known in the world of haute couture before she was forced to take up her duty and marry Gregor. "When I was at the draper's in Istanbul yesterday, I happened on a wonderful silk."

"If it was so wonderful, why didn't you purchase it then?"

"Because I was busy getting ready for the show." She stopped and shook her head, for since the King had died her life had been a whirlwind of change.

He stared at the gown for a long solemn moment, the beautifully chiseled lines of his face revealing no emotion. She fidgeted with her hands, uncertain what else she could say to convince that this froth of satin, lace and beads was all wrong for her.

"How long will it take you to make this design of yours?" he asked, neither agreeing with her request or denying it.

"A week at the most."

"Do you always work that fast?"

"Most of the time." And often late into the night, losing time as she became engrossed in a project. "One more thing. All of my clothes and personal belongings are at my flat in Athens. I need to have my partner send them here."

He stroked the arrogant line of his jaw and stared at her so long she felt sweat dot her forehead and dampen the undersides of her breasts. "Very well. Phone your partner and have your things readied," he said. "A courier will pick them up this afternoon and deliver them here by tonight."

She smiled and retrieved her phone from her bag, too excited over being allowed to make her gown to feel annoyance that he listened to her every word.

With her call ended, she slid her phone on the table and jotted down the address to her flat. She handed that to him with a grateful smile. "Thank you. You won't regret it."

"Come now—you can do better than that," he said.

She felt the sudden change in him as he strode toward her with predatory intent, as if she'd just issued a challenge he couldn't refuse.

"What do you mean?" She backed up, suddenly desperate

to keep him at arm's reach when her body ached to do the opposite.

"I've just granted you your wish. This concession certainly deserves more than a mere thank-you."

Her backside hit the wall and slammed a startled squeak from her. But he didn't stop advancing until he was inches from her, so close her body burned from the heat radiating off his.

Any coherent thought she might have had vanished. All she could think of was how much she wanted him to kiss her. Hold her. Love her?

The intensity in his gaze changed, sparking a new emotion in his eyes. Before she could read its meaning he reached out and sifted his fingers through her hair, from the scalp to the ends that reached nearly to her waist.

"Your hair is like dark rich coffee, and holds highlights of the deepest sea and midnight sun, yet against the white it simply looks black."

She froze in place, the gentle pull on her scalp tugging at emotions she kept carefully hidden. Yet she couldn't deny the thread of energy that passed from him to her, tightening to draw her closer.

She tried to push him away, both palms on his chest, refusing to allow that to happen. But touching him was the wrong thing to do too.

For now she felt the beat of his heart, strong and sure, beneath her hand. The solid wall of his chest was as unyielding as the man, yet so hot that her own skin began to heat.

Sensual fire blazed in his dark eyes and her lungs felt scorched, too tight to draw breath. She burned in other places too, and a silent gathering of moisture between her thighs and the tightening of her core muscles proved her body responded on its own to his potent virility.

She hated him for waking her needs with just a look, for making her want him. Crave his touch.

Before she could think of a pithy retort to end this madness, he smiled at her. Any hint of cruelty was gone, replaced by something that took her breath away, something that reminded her of the carefree man she'd first met.

It was really nothing more than a slight curling of his sensuous lips, a knowing smirk like the gods had bestowed upon women. A telling look that told her he was well aware of just how much he affected her, that let her know he was in control, that he could tempt her to do more if he wished.

The puppeteer pulling the strings on the marionette.

Yet she couldn't find the energy or the anger to do more than drop her hands from his chest.

It was enough for her to make a stand, to lift her chin in silent defiance. But her body defied her again, for her breasts felt heavier, straining toward him, the nipples unbearably tight and aching.

"So soft," he said, grazing her lower lip with his thumb until it was full and tingling. His fingers skimmed down the curve of her jaw, stirring the fire of desire in her. "The sun has kissed your skin just enough to make it glow."

Was that a compliment? Even if it was praising her in a good way, she didn't care.

He splayed one hand on the wall by her head, while his thumb continued its meandering path down her neck to rest on the upper swells of her breasts. A pulse pounded in her throat and between her thighs, leaving her tingling with want. With a need so great she could barely draw a breath.

"You are lovely beyond words," he said, his voice dropping to a crushed-velvet baritone that strummed her taut nerves in an erotic melody.

Demi managed a smile, and knew anything more would be a struggle. It had been a year since he'd held her prisoner by a smoldering look. She hadn't been able to break free then. She didn't think she could now. She didn't know if she even wanted to try.

But she couldn't stand here either, and let him stroke her neck and her arm and the heaving upper swells of her bosom. She couldn't let him make love to her with his eyes when he held her in such contempt in his heart.

She grasped his thick wrists and tried to tug his hands from her. "Please. Don't do this."

"Why, when it is something we both take pleasure in?" His palms cupped her breasts with a familiarity that shocked her, that brought to aching life all the feelings she'd held deep in the night.

Her hands slid up his muscular arms to find purchase in the hard muscles as he weighed each one, before his hands bracketed her torso, flinging her back to that day on the beach when she'd granted a stranger far too much liberty because she'd been powerless to stop herself. Because she'd been so hungry for love.

But where she'd lacked the strength of will then, pride gave her a modicum of strength now.

"Stop it," she said, trying to push his hands from her and failing, humiliated he could make her want him so badly that she'd let him have his way with her.

Kristo ignored her protests and continued his exploration. "You have lost weight."

It angered her that he could tell the differences in her from before. Infuriated her that her body ached to sway into his.

His hands slid to her waist and her fingers closed over his, trying to stop him, trying not to feel anything but hatred and anger that he was putting her through this torment.

"I've worked long hard hours of late, in preparation for the Athens show." Time and energy wasted now, for she wouldn't be allowed to participate in it. "Something a royal would know nothing of."

His palms cupped her bottom and pulled her flush against his length. "Are you insinuating that I live a life of leisure? Because I can assure you that I too put in long hard hours working."

Her breath caught, for the hard length of his desire was pressed against her belly. His arousal should disgust her, but her body melted and bowed into him, wanting him.

"Yes, I've seen pictures of you in the tabloids, hard at work for Angyra," she said, her chin lifted in defiance.

Each time she'd seen him linked with a new woman she'd been bitten with unwanted jealousy. On its heels had always come anger for allowing herself to be seduced by him in the first place.

The sensual mouth that had curled into a mesmerizing smile now pulled into a hard line. She knew she'd struck a nerve, and clearly one that was raw.

He pushed away from her so quickly that she stumbled to catch her balance, but he didn't notice. He was already halfway to the door.

"As I said, the wedding takes place in twelve days," he said.

"I'll have the gown finished in one week."

He paused at the door and glanced back at her. "I will approve the design before you begin, understand?"

She bobbed her head. "Of course."

He gave her another exacting perusal that had her skin tingling with awareness again. "I will send a servant up to assist you."

"I'd prefer my own assistants."

Again that slash of white teeth against dark skin, the cocky smile of a shark who had his quarry cornered. Or so he thought.

"I am sure that you would," he said. "But you will have to make do with what I provide for you."

Without waiting to see if she'd argue or concede, he swept from the room and closed the door in his wake. Such arrogance!

How would she ever cope with this man? Being with him rattled her senses so much she'd forgotten to tell Yannis everything that she'd need.

She reached for her phone—but it wasn't there. How odd. She'd finished talking to Yannis and laid it there. She hadn't touched it again the entire time Kristo had been in her room.

Kristo! He must have taken it.

She ran to the door he'd just left by, intending to go after him. The unmistakable click of the lock froze her in place. He'd locked her in. And that drove home the fact that she wasn't simply the bride-to-be. She was a prisoner—not just in the palace but in this room.

Kristo was firmly in control of her. He was smug in his belief that she could do nothing but blindly follow his orders, that she'd melt at his touch.

And to her shame she *had*—every time. She'd never lost control around any man but him. Though she'd believed it had been a fluke, that she'd resist him if ever they met again, she now knew that wasn't true.

Her face flamed with anger and embarrassment. How could one man make her toss aside her convictions? How could he make her want him when she hated the very air he breathed?

"Damn you!" she screamed, venting the anger inside her.

But it wasn't enough.

So, because she could, because he'd left her no other recourse after treating her like a dockside trollop being passed from one brother to the next, she crossed to the lavish gown that had been made for her.

Gregor had never sought her opinion. Neither had Kristo. Neither would ever have done so.

She suffered one moment of indecision, for the gown had certainly cost a fortune. That was her. Always thinking of the other person's feelings—in this case a designer she didn't even know.

She had always done what was required of her, from her papa to the King. And look where it had gotten her!

Locked in a room in a palace and forced to marry a man who despised her.

Quite simply, she looked at the stark white gown and saw red.

With anger pounding through her veins in thick molten waves, she ripped the heavy overskirt off the gown. The mile-long train came next, followed by the grossly puffed sleeves.

She yanked and ripped and reduced most of the gown to rags.

It was petulant. Wasteful. Destructive. But it proved one thing.

She, too, could only be pushed so far.

He shouldn't have touched her. Touched?

Ha! Kristo paced the length of his private salon and battled the lust that throbbed through him, begging for release. He'd done far more than touch Demetria Andreou. His hands had molded over the lush swell of her breasts in a blatant caress, lingering until her nipples budded against his palm, until his sex grew to an unrelenting ache.

For that brief moment time had stood still. He'd been back on the beach with her. Both wet from the surf. Both hot with desire.

Just like then he'd easily gotten lost, stroking the gentle curves of her torso and waist, relearning her shape even though every delicious inch was branded on his memory. The shivers that had danced over her silken skin and into him in an erotic rhythm had pounded in his soul.

He'd pushed resentment and anger from his mind. He'd forgotten who she was. Forgotten they were bound by duty.

He had simply been a man caressing a very desirable woman. A woman who responded to him as no other ever had.

And that was the problem. All he had to do was touch her and he went up like dry kindling, the fires of desire roaring through him so hotly that they burned out all reason.

He could barely think beyond the driving need to sate the hunger that gnawed within him. And now that she was here in the palace—now that they were alone...

This time Kristo had to finish what he'd started with her a year ago. Maybe then he could be near her without being consumed by this primitive lust.

He wanted her. He'd have her. But he'd be a fool to trust her.

The door to his suite opened and Vasos slipped inside, deceptively quiet for such a giant of a man. That was why he was the best bodyguard a man could want.

He could move soundlessly. He could blend in. And Kristo trusted him with his life. Now he trusted him with Demetria's as well.

"Your Majesty," Vasos said, and bowed. He rarely let emotion show on his rugged face. But right now that visage was drawn in deep lines of worry.

"What's wrong?" he asked.

"Demetria has destroyed the royal wedding gown."

"How?"

His mouth turned down. "She ripped it apart with her bare hands."

He'd have never thought her capable of such rage. Such volatile passion.

Anger curdled in Kristo, but he couldn't help but allow a grim smile as well. She would need a strong hand. A man who could match her in bed and out!

"The lady is removing the options," he said.

Vasos lifted one thick black eyebrow, the action far more noticeable due to his cleanly shaven head. "I don't understand."

"She is a clothing designer." A very angry one, because she hadn't been consulted about her wedding gown.

She didn't trust him to abide by his promise either. So she had removed his choice. She played to win.

"I was not aware of her vocation," Vasos said.

He likely never would have been either if Gregor hadn't fallen ill and passed the crown and the lady over into his care. Damn, what a coil!

"Alert the guards to pay close watch on the palace. Keeping her under lock and key will only breed more resentment." She certainly resented him enough already! "I don't wish for Demetria to leave it as yet."

"As you wish, Your Majesty." Vasos bowed and then left the room.

Kristo stared at the closed door for the longest time. In the span of a few days his life had turned into a complication. Duty. Business. Desire.

He'd gone from second son to Crown Prince to King in just one day's time. Now he'd soon add husband to that list.

Kristo crossed to the window that afforded a magnificent view of the mountains. But the peace he usually derived from admiring this vista was lost on him today.

Destiny had brought him and Demetria together again.

Only the gods knew if it would be a marriage made in heaven or hell.

His door opened and closed, and he cast a brief glance at his younger brother.

"She's gorgeous," Mikhael said, shunning greetings to get to the heart of the matter, as always.

"She's the same woman who visited here one year ago," he said, and realized that though that might be true he hadn't truly known her then. He wasn't certain he knew her now.

"Perhaps." Mikhael strode to the wet bar and splashed whiskey in a glass. "Did she balk at the prospect of marrying you?"

He heard the underlying humor in his brother's voice and smiled. "She had no choice."

"A leech then, eager to latch on to to the next in line so she can have a plush life?"

Exactly what he'd thought. But then he pictured what Vasos had told him and burst into laughter. "More like a barracuda caught in our nets. She reduced her wedding gown to ribbons because she hated it."

"A feisty one, then," Mikhael said. "At least your marriage should be somewhat entertaining."

"It will surely be the most talked about wedding in decades." Kristo's thoughts turned to his ill brother. "Have you heard from Gregor?"

"He's checked into a hospital in Athens. I dislike him being alone, so I intend to go there after I conclude my business in London."

"A business or pleasure trip?"

"A bit of both." Mikhael finished his drink and set the heavy glass on the marble counter. "Call if you need me."

"That goes both ways." For if Gregor's health took a sudden turn for the worse he wanted to know. He wanted to be by his brother's side.

He waited until Mikhael had left the room before crossing to the bar. He poured a generous portion of ouzo in a glass and took a sip, savoring the taste of anise on his tongue.

Demetria was not at all what he'd expected. He'd thought her to be a shameless flirt, yet she dreamed of pursuing a career as a designer. She had goals and wants beyond duty.

In that they were the same. But as the King his days would be crowded with state functions and problems, as well as the mundane duties that came with so heavy an obligation.

His life would no longer be his own. What little peace he found would be here in this house with his family.

"A man should love his wife," his mother had told him. And he allowed that was true.

He'd never wanted a union like his parents had had, which was why he was still very much single. Why he'd thought to remain that way until he was at least forty. Until he'd found the one woman who would share his dreams and desires.

But he'd already bored of the nightlife that Mikhael still favored. Having a different beauty on his arm and in his bed had grown as tiresome as the dearth of conversation he'd had with those socialites.

He wanted a woman who was real, who cared about this country and him. Dammit, he wanted Demetria Andreou.

CHAPTER THREE

WITH her rare display of temper ended, and the reality of her situation resting heavily on her, Demi dug into her bag for her sketchpad and pencil.

In less than two weeks she'd be Queen of Angyra. She'd come to accept that fate, which put an end to her career before it had truly even begun. But her entire being was tossed into turmoil when she realized that she'd be Kristo's wife.

A chill ribboned through her, more troubling than ever before. For while she'd seen herself as a convenient wife to Gregor, she knew there would be nothing well suited about an alliance between her and Kristo.

Unless she counted passion.

And that was the last thing she wished to dwell on now!

Angry with herself for her lapse of good judgment where Kristo was concerned, she grabbed her sketchpad and pencil and moved to the chaise positioned by the bank of tall windows. With any luck she'd lose herself in her work.

She certainly needed a mental escape now! But while she'd done hundreds of sketches, perhaps more if she counted the doodles made without forethought, she hadn't designed a wedding gown since her days at university.

Those fanciful sketches born from a girl on the cusp of womanhood had eventually been transformed into a woman's fondest dream. Quick sketches of how she'd wanted her own royal wedding to be, right down to the handsome prince by her side.

Except when that time had drawn near her prince had selected her gown for her.

Everything had been planned without consulting her.

She'd known there would have been no love in her marriage to Gregor. No happily ever after looming in her future. But she'd expected respect.

Now she knew that wouldn't have happened either.

Kristo was little better.

Yes, he desired her. But for how long? When would he tire of his Queen and seek comfort elsewhere?

That thought unsettled her more than she wished to admit. She'd never seen a picture of him in a tabloid without an accompanying beauty on his arm.

The playboy prince had frequented every hot resort in the world. His contemporaries were the filthy rich—those who made a living playing.

Yet she'd met him on a deserted beach, where he'd been working to protect sea turtles.

The two images of the man were at odds. A contradiction that defied explanation.

He'd shown a different side of himself then that she hadn't seen since. It was almost as if she'd dreamed him up. A mysterious Titan from the sea who passionately guarded his world and the creatures in it. Her as well?

She shook off that disturbing thought and put pencil to paper, letting desire guide her strokes as she sketched the design she'd envisioned all of her life. If she had any hope of convincing him of her talent then her gown had to be unique. Totally her.

The lines and details must showcase her figure and what she believed would fire the desires of an arrogantly handsome King. If she could achieve both, her gown would be talked about for years. She would forever be listed as an innovative designer who'd given up her career for royal life.

A sad smile played over her mouth when she realized how she'd just romanticized her fate. If only she had been given choices. If only the Crown Prince had courted her, tried to win her heart.

Minutes slipped into hours.

She'd just put the finishing touches to the sketch of her dream gown when a key jingling in the lock broke her concentration. She looked up just as a young woman slipped inside the room, with garments draped over her arm. Vasos was right behind her, carrying a wicker basket teeming with bottles and delicate vials, his rugged face drawn in stoic lines.

The maid scampered off into a room that Demetria had yet to explore. She'd assumed it was likely a bedroom or a dressing chamber. As she had no desire to sleep and no clothes to change into, she had remained in this room.

A room that was twice the size of her flat! But of all the seating areas in this room she preferred staying in what had been provided as a work area.

"The King requests your presence for dinner at eight." Vasos set the basket of sundries down. "He has selected these fragrances and potions for your pleasure."

"How good of him to release me from my prison," she said, but curiosity goaded her to sort through the array of bottles to see what Kristo thought would suit her. "Is this to be a private dinner or will there be guests?"

"Private," he said. "You will be dining on the terrace."

"An informal meal, then?"

The guard inclined his bald head in agreement.

Good. Her nerves were too jangled to be presented to guests as yet. And yet the thought of dining alone with Kristo did nothing to ease her mind either.

"Either a servant or I will come for you at a quarter of eight," Vasos said.

"Thank you."

Vasos left. The click of the lock in the door signaled she'd be left in peace again.

Peace? She wondered if she'd ever be at peace again.

She'd been willing to do her duty, but she'd also thought she'd have time to live the life she'd dreamed off as well. Now she was reduced to haggling for the opportunity to create her own wedding gown!

Demi bit her lower lip, admitting only to herself that her anxiety went beyond her duty to marry. She'd never set out to betray Gregor. Her attraction to Kristo was simply too powerful for her to resist.

Afterward she'd walked on pins and needles, certain that at any moment the King would demand an audience with her. That Kristo would tell all of his encounter with her on the beach. That she'd be deemed unfaithful. Unworthy of the title of Queen.

That she'd be banned from the kingdom.

That she'd be free to embark on her career as a designer.

But it hadn't happened that way then, or after she'd returned to the university to finish her studies.

Kristo had held their secret. Why?

She knew the reason for her own secrecy. Though she'd wanted nothing more than to be free of her obligation to the crown, she'd known that jilting the Crown Prince would carry severe repercussions.

She'd have been fodder for the gossip mills. That alone had stopped her, for she refused to follow in her mother's footsteps. She wouldn't mirror her shame.

Demi wouldn't live up to the name whispered behind her back when she was only six—*scandal's daughter*.

She'd rather live silently with the guilt of her actions.

Ah, easier said than done.

Demi retrieved her sketchpad and returned to the chaise, desperate to push her troubles from her mind if only for an hour. She couldn't change what had been done.

But perhaps she could have a hand in shaping her own future.

The design she'd just sketched was beautiful, the lines clean and crisp. Yet this design had been done through the eyes of the naïve woman she'd once been. A romantic gown that would showcase her love.

Except there was no love in her upcoming marriage.

But then she wasn't that naïve girl anymore either.

She'd ceased being her the day she'd met Kristo Stanrakis.

It was time she was completely true to the crown. To her future husband. And finally to herself.

With that in mind, she quickly set to work on a new design. There wasn't time to complete it, but she could at least make a few rough drawings. Surely one of them would suit the bride of duty?

Kristo jammed both hands in his trouser pockets and paced the length of the terrace. He was not used to waiting for a woman and he disliked doing so now.

In fact this was the first time he'd been made to wait, for the ladies of his acquaintance were eager to please him—to gain his favor. Not so Demetria.

Duty bound them together. But would it and this sizzling desire be enough to keep them together?

It must. He refused to fail in his marriage. Refused to fail his family and his kingdom.

His body tensed, sensing her near even before he caught a whiff of her perfume. Before he heard the rapid click of high heels on the cypress wood floors.

He turned just as she stepped onto the terrace. Seeing her backlit in a wash of light simply took his breath away.

She wore a slinky strapless dress the color of pomegranates that hugged her luscious curves. No jewelry other than a slim gold wristwatch.

Her hair hung straight and long, a silken waterfall of dark strands that caught and reflected the light. His fingers itched to run through it. If she wore make-up at all, it was just the barest hint of eyeshadow and a kiss of tanned glimmer on the sensuous bow of her lips.

There was no artifice about her. Nothing intently provocative. Yet she oozed sex appeal. His body answered with the throb of awakening desire that pounded through him.

"You look lovely," he said.

A smile briefly trembled on her lips, proof that a case of nerves gripped her as well. But where he could hide his behind a stern mask, the emotions on her face were as exposed as the creamy slope of her neck and shoulders that pebbled under his scrutiny.

"Thank you," she said, managing to compose herself quickly and assume a regal mien.

She clearly had the advantage, for she'd been groomed to be Queen. She was aware of her role, even if she was uncertain of the man she was to marry.

But this life he'd been thrust into was all uncharted waters to him. He'd been as reluctant to accept his fate as the people were to trust him.

On Angyra gossip moved as hot and quickly as a Sirocco, and left tempers just as strained. He was well aware of the whispers that his past exploits would hinder the crown.

There was much speculation among the people as to whether he was capable of leading. He had his own doubts and fears, for he was ill-prepared for this role. He was the second son. The spare who'd grown up in the Crown Prince's shadow.

The man who'd served his country with reckless fervor, gaining allies abroad and censure within Angyra.

Now the weight of the kingdom rested heavily on his shoulders. He'd replaced the favored son. Now he'd claim Gregor's bride as well!

As far as his libido went, that couldn't come soon enough. And why should he wait?

He took a step toward her without conscious thought. "I trust you approve of the garments provided?"

"It was really too much," she said, taking a step back.

"Feel free to send back anything you dislike."

Her eyes widened and her lips parted ever so slightly, as if she hadn't expected him to be that generous. "I'm used to wearing my own designs."

"That isn't necessary any longer."

"But I prefer to. Surely there is no harm in that?"

He was tempted to applaud the manner in which she smoothly kept the conversation on the subject most dear to her heart—the career she was giving up for the crown. She would likely gain much sympathy if that tidbit was released to the press.

It would certainly elevate the people's love for her even more. Though he wanted her to hold favor with them, he didn't wish to do so at the expense of his own shaky reputation.

That was badly tainted already, for the majority still saw him as the playboy prince. He was the spoilt son who'd whiled his time and fortune away at gaming tables across the world.

He'd lived in the fast lane, enjoying a decadent life, while his brother had remained at the palace seeing to the needs of the people. Or at least that was how it appeared.

Only a handful of people were aware that he'd been responsible for the elevated working conditions at the Chrysos Mine. That he'd worked secretly for the good of his country. And that was how he wished it to remain. He didn't want praise for what had needed to be done.

With his own funds he'd bought deserted beaches. He'd ensured that they'd remain a national preserve for the benefit of the endangered sea turtles as well as other wildlife.

On one of those beaches he and Demetria had surrendered to passion. It was hard to believe the poised woman now garbed in the latest fashion was the same woman he'd held in his arms.

He longed to rip away the pretense. To strip them of lies and duty and just revel in the desire that raged between them.

"Why do you insist on working when your duties will command the majority of your time?"

"Surely being the Queen will not take up every waking minute."

"Have you forgotten your role as my wife?"

Without waiting for her to answer, he lifted her hand and placed a kiss on the satin skin. The jolt that tore through her mirrored his own reaction to being near her.

"How could I?" She pulled her hand back as if she'd been burned.

"I'm glad you finally understand that designers will clamor for *your* attention."

She hiked her chin up, cheeks flushed and lips thinned. "Then I'll make certain I'm seen wearing my partner's creations."

He bit back a grim smile. No doubt her own ideas would find their way into those garments as well. Fine! If that appeased her, then so be it.

But it was clear her choice went beyond simple likes and dislikes. Her favoritism would certainly boost her partner's career.

Again, there was nothing wrong in that.

Her loyalty to her partner was admirable. Pity she hadn't held been that faithful to the Crown Prince!

He strode to the liquor cart. "Would you like a drink?"

"Chablis would be nice," she said. "Where are your servants and bodyguards?"

"The servants will deliver the food in due time. As for guards—there is no need for them to dog my steps inside the palace."

He poured a glass of wine for her, and chose *tsipouro* over ice for himself. This was the first time he'd been totally alone with her since that day on the beach.

Unlike then, there was nothing welcoming in the cool gaze she fixed on him. There was no wonder at watching nature unfold reflected in her eyes that were the color of mocha, at finding pleasure in each other's arms.

No, there was only a keen sense of wariness that bubbled between them.

He didn't trust her. She clearly didn't like him.

It was not the way to start a marriage.

But then theirs wasn't a union based on emotion or attraction. Duty forced them together. Forced him to be bound to his brother's betrothed—a woman who hadn't hesitated to betray Gregor.

No, all they had in common was smoldering desire. To his annoyance that had only grown stronger. But would it abate once they finally sated this driving need?

Would they then become like his own parents? Two people who had rarely spoken to each other, who for the most part had lived separate lives?

"I didn't realize we'd be alone," she said, her soft voice holding a quaver of uncertainty now.

He pressed the glass into her hand, noting the increased pulse in her slender neck. "Does being with me sans guests make you nervous?"

"Of course not!"

"You are not a good liar."

She set her glass aside without touching a drop of the vintage wine. "Very well. I'm uncomfortable being around someone who thinks so ill of me."

"How can you expect me to do anything but? You were unfaithful to my brother! You broke your betrothal vows."

"With you!"

A cynical snort ripped from him. "Ah, so now *I* am to blame for your lapse of morals?"

She crossed her arms over her chest, looking hurt and proud at the same time. "I refuse to discuss this, for you've already made up your narrow mind to paint me as a floozy when you were the one who seduced me."

He paused, for in truth he had done just that. He'd seen a beautiful woman and gone after her.

She'd seen him as a man—not a prince, not a rich man who could better her life. She'd seemed fascinated by the work he was doing, and that was the most potent turn-on he'd ever experienced.

"You could have said no," he said, but guilt had served to strip his tone of its caustic bite.

She shook her head, looking shamed. Miserable. Guilty. "I tried, but simply couldn't."

At least she was honest about the powerful magnetic pull of desire that had yet to lose its strength for either of them. "What is done is done. There is no sense rehashing it."

She walked to the railing, her back straight and her shoulders held tight. "There's just one thing I must know. Why didn't you tell Gregor about us?"

Such a simple question, and yet so damned hard to answer. "I was certain Gregor and the King would believe that I was as much at fault as you."

"So you held your tongue for selfish reasons. My God, you

only think of your own needs. You don't respect my wishes. My desires."

"Respect? You've done nothing to earn my respect." He tossed back his liquor and slammed the glass down, but the memory of that moment with her in his arms refused to dim.

"Nor have you done anything to earn mine!"

He stalked toward her, backing her up against the railing. Moving close to her until there was barely a breath of air between them. Until he breathed in her floral scent tinged with anger.

He caught her chin under a bent finger and nudged her face up to him, thinking a man could drown in her turbulent eyes. "Why do you persist in placing the blame on me?"

"Because during the ten years I was betrothed to Gregor we should have known each other." She batted his hand away and slipped from him, her narrowed gaze glittering with censure. "Of course for that to have happened you would have to have been in attendance more than the first time I visited Angyra."

Of course she'd shift the blame back to him again! Did she really think he'd believe she'd kept her head in the sand all these years? That she'd been out of touch with the events of the world in the months preceding her last visit to Angyra?

"The fact remains I had not seen you since you were twelve years old," he said, and let his gaze run admiringly over her curvaceous form once more. "You have changed considerably."

"As have you," she shot back.

"Yet I can't believe you never saw my name or my picture in countless gossip magazines," he said.

Everywhere he'd turned over the years, especially in that tense time frame, he'd seen himself and a woman he'd had a brief affair with emblazoned on every cover. The fickle woman who'd failed to tell him that she was married. Who was responsible for him vowing to avoid marriage until he was at least forty—for he'd been sure it would take that long before he'd ever trust a woman again.

And then he'd met Demetria.

The object of his desire and anger wrinkled her pert nose, as if even the thought of being aware of such celebrity news was distasteful. "I never read them—even when I see them clustered on the news racks."

He had trouble believing that. His father had never read those magazines either, and yet he'd been well aware of the vicious gossip that had ensnared Kristo and the married woman. Hell, everyone on Angyra knew of his dalliance!

The King had been so enraged by his conduct that he'd threatened to remove him from his duties to the crown. But while he wouldn't have minded having someone else take over the role of ambassador, Kristo had refused to relinquish his position safeguarding Angyra's natural treasures, which included the Chrysos Mine.

He'd had to talk long and hard to convince the King to give him another chance. And that was why he'd kept his mouth shut about him and Demetria.

Yes, she was right. His reasons were selfish—but not entirely the ones she believed.

"It was in Angyra's best interests to let the matter of our tryst remain secret," he said.

"Angyra's interests or your own?"

He swirled the liquor in his glass, the chink of ice loud in the ensuing silence. She persisted in thinking the worst of him while seeing herself as the one put upon.

Yet in this they were alike. They were both passionate about their personal interests. Both at fault.

"What of you, Demetria? It is obvious you place your career

above your duty," he said, and had the satisfaction of seeing her body stiffen in silent admission.

Ah, that was her sore spot. Her career. Wasn't it said that the artistic crowd were a sensitive lot when it came to their craft?

She certainly was defensive of her desire to be a designer. Yet if that were true, why hadn't she taken the easy way out when she'd had the chance?

"If you had confessed what you'd done, the King would have been eager to release you from your betrothal contract," he said, watching her closely now that he'd put her on the spot. "Gregor certainly wouldn't have wished to have anything to do with you."

"Or with you?" she countered.

"You are a fine one to talk when you are consumed with this notion of designing clothes," he said. "Why did *you* keep what we'd done secret?"

She refused to look at him, which only convinced him that she wouldn't be forthcoming with the truth. "My father would have been enraged."

No doubt that was true, yet with her career unfolding she could have managed well without him. "There must be more to it than that."

"There wasn't."

Yes, she was still lying to him. But why? What was she hiding?

"Enough talk about the career you failed to grasp when you had the chance," he said. "First and foremost you are groomed to be Queen. Nothing more."

Her features looked as smooth and cold as porcelain. "I am well aware of my duty, Your Majesty. I only ask to be allowed to design my wedding gown. Are you denying me that now as well?"

He stared at her, sorely tempted to pull her flush against

him and prove that she would respond freely to his touch. That this tension that sizzled between them was as much born from pent-up desire as from anger and a good dose of frustration.

"Go ahead and create your wedding gown," he said. "Let it be your one shining moment in the design world."

"I will." Affecting a dismissal that would have done his mother proud, she whirled and strode to the door.

"Where are you going?"

"To my room." She flung it open, and then paused to look back at him. "I've lost my appetite. Do forgive me."

She strode out without waiting for his permission.

Kristo fumed silently, torn between going after her and letting the matter drop for tonight. Enough had been said already.

Duty bound them together, just as it had generations of kings and queens of Angyra.

Like any delicate business endeavor, he must handle Demetria diplomatically. Twelve days seemed an eternity before he could claim her as he longed to do.

He was not one who sat around waiting for events to unfold. He struck first. He *made* things happen, for then he was in control.

This was no different.

He wanted her, and he wasn't above seducing her into his arms. Next time she wouldn't walk away from him.

CHAPTER FOUR

THE sun was just peeking above the verdant mountains that lay black and sleeping by the time Demi finished sketching the design for her wedding gown. It had taken her two attempts before she'd finally envisioned a gown that suited her.

At least she had something to be proud of for her night's work. Something that she could present to the King of Arrogance today.

Just thinking of him set her insides quivering anew, just as they'd been when she'd returned to her room last night. She'd been so furious with his high-handedness that she could have screamed.

Yet that anger had been tempered when she'd returned to find that her personal effects had been delivered in her absence. And that wasn't the only surprise.

A sewing machine, serger and a variety of sundries she'd requested had also been set up, creating a studio that outshone the one she had in Athens. A studio that was a designer's dream.

For a long moment she'd just stood there, stunned that Kristo had kept his promise. That everything she'd need was right at her disposal.

In that exhilarating spate of time she'd been on the verge of rushing back to the terrace to thank Kristo.

But sanity had prevailed—for she'd known in her heart if

she did that she'd not return to her room that night. She'd end up in his arms. In his bed.

She'd not find the willpower to break free of him a second time. Already she was weary of fighting the inevitable.

But she was determined to gain the upper hand over this raging desire. She had to. She would not let her passions control her, weaken her, as they had surely ruled her mother!

In less than two weeks she'd be the Queen of this country. She'd be Kristo's wife. But though she was giving up her career, she refused to lose the essence of who she was.

She studied her new sketch with a critical eye. It was a blend of modern and traditional lines purely from her imagination. New. A bit daring.

This reflected the woman she was now, not the fanciful girl she'd been.

The dream gown of a woman.

A design nobody had ever seen. A style that people would remember forever for the romantic vein it captured while still looking sophisticated.

It was a very simple classical design, with a delicate golden-embroidered edging on the bell skirt. A nearly sheer lace cream shawl shot with gold softened a simple strapless bodice and lent a seductively mysterious air.

The ivory color would complement her light olive complexion. The addition of gold would set it apart from the majority of gowns.

And that touch of gold would lessen its appeal to the masses who wanted virginal white or palest cream. It would set the bride too far from tradition.

Her shoulders slumped as that fact hit home.

For that reason alone she feared the King would dismiss it straight away. He'd likely want a more opulent style, encrusted with pearls. A style that screamed wealth and old world and was totally unlike her. Something in the order of the lavish gown Gregor had commissioned.

She rubbed her forehead, unable to think clearly anymore. She crossed to the sofa on legs that feel wooden.

She desperately needed sleep, and if she was lucky she would be too exhausted to dream of one tall, arrogant King.

Kristo let himself into Demetria's room midmorning, with the intention of asking her to join him for a walk. He wanted to get her away from the palace for a while. He wanted to start over fresh with her before they embarked on this arranged marriage.

But his impatience to put the strained past behind them froze when he caught sight of her curled on the sofa, fast asleep. She looked like an angel, with her dark hair spilling to the floor and her long lashes sweeping her sun-kissed cheeks.

He frowned, noting the darker smudges beneath her eyes. Had she stayed up all night?

He noticed the sketchpad lying on the table, as well as the pages ripped out and lying helter-skelter. Some were of completed gowns. Others were clearly half-formed ideas that she'd discarded for one reason or another.

The one finished design on the sketchpad caught his attention. The detailing was minute, with neatly printed notes explaining the finer points.

He could picture her wearing it and knew she'd turn all heads her way. She'd surely capture *his* attention with her creamy shoulders covered with only the sheerest strip of cloth kissed with threads of gold.

Kristo's gaze lifted to Demetria, lost in sleep. He wasn't a stranger to working all night and grabbing a nap when he could. But he hadn't thought she would work this hard to create a design for her wedding gown. He hadn't thought she was this dedicated.

Again, she wasn't behaving like the conniving woman he'd envisioned. What other surprises would he discover about her?

He paused at the sofa and reached down to slide his hand beneath the dark hair falling over the pillow. His fingers slipped through the mass as if it were spun silk—another memory that had tormented him.

He'd toyed with a woman's hair before, but he'd never felt this deep erotic pull. Never been so distracted by a woman. Never had his pulse quicken and his breath catch just watching her sleep.

He knew her hair and body held the scent of exotic flowers and the sea. He'd been tormented by the brief memory of those long strands brushing against his naked body. But he wanted more. He wanted to bury his hands in her hair when they were in the throes of passion. When he finally made her his.

How much he'd thrill to have her glorious hair blanket them both after they'd sated their need, to sink into her again.

His mouth thinned. She'd lost a night's sleep with her sketches, but his inability to get her out of his thoughts had deprived him of the same for nearly a year.

At this moment he was in the same uncomfortable place he'd been before he'd sought sleep—wanting her with a ravenous hunger. Surely that overwhelming need would be sated once they'd made love. Once she was his and his alone.

She wouldn't invade his thoughts during the day. She wouldn't weave in and out of his dreams at night.

Eleven days before the royal wedding. It seemed a lifetime away.

Kristo let her dark hair fall from his fingers to the pillow, impatient to get her alone. To claim her as his own.

He crossed to the sketches again, no longer taking care to be quiet. Her talent was remarkable. She surely would have made a name for herself among the top designers.

Her soft gasp ribboned toward him on a sense of earthy awareness. "How long have you been here?"

"Only a few minutes." He canted the sketchpad her way. "Is this the design you favor?"

She huddled in the corner of the sofa, a fringed throw drawn around her, cheeks tinged a dusty coral that emphasized the dark half-moon smudges beneath her luminous eyes. Eyes that were surely red-rimmed, proving she hadn't been asleep long.

"Yes. What do you think?"

That her talent was unparalleled. That while Angyra gained a Queen, the world of fashion would lose a budding star.

"It's nice," he said instead. "If your ability to sew is as good as your talent for design, you will certainly be the most gorgeous bride that Angyra has ever had."

A deeper flush stole over her cheeks, giving him the impression she was unused to such compliments. "I'm relieved you approve. With your permission, I'll return to the draper in Istanbul and select the cloth."

He shrugged and dropped the sketchpad on the table, where it landed with a muffled thud.

"It's out of the question for you to travel alone."

Her brow pulled into a deep frown. "Are you always this controlling?"

"I am always this cautious."

"What a convenient answer."

"You are the bride-to-be of the King of Angyra," he said. "From now on you don't leave the palace without a bodyguard."

She slumped back against the sofa and hugged her arms against her pert breasts like a petulant child might do, but the pensive glance she cast out the window confirmed she hadn't considered the need for high security.

"I've always been free to come and go." She shook her head and lifted her gaze to his, a storm of annoyance brewing in her eyes. "How do you adjust to the loss of privacy?"

He gave an impatient shrug. "You are asking me something I have never known—not as you have."

Her lips firmed in a tight line and a chill glinted in her eyes. "Of course—what was I thinking? A man of privilege would have no idea how the other half lives."

He muttered a curse, for she'd hit on a hot button of his own. It was the main reason he'd fought for his role as ambassador. It had carried him away from Angyra and the stiff formality that ruled in the palace.

In Cannes or Vegas or Rio he had been able to mingle with people to a degree. He had lived a somewhat normal life even though he'd had a bodyguard shadowing him.

But that role was history, for his duty now was as King of this kingdom. He had to be more careful. He could no longer take a night on the town without a horde of reporters or, worse, political adversaries of Angyra following him.

His wife would be obliged to be just as circumspect.

"The palace isn't a prison, Demetria," he said, and swore again, for his father had said much the same to him years ago.

"But our marriage will be a life sentence unless—"

"Do not say it!" His gaze shot to hers, and he didn't try to hide the anger burning in his soul for it masked a greater fear. "There has never been a divorce in the Royal House of Stanrakis, and I won't break that tradition with you."

"I wasn't suggesting that!"

He threaded his fingers through his hair. This topic was scraping his nerves raw. Nothing could be gained from bemoaning their fate. Nothing.

"You are not the only one who isn't pleased with this arranged marriage, but this country has seen enough unrest with my father's sudden death followed by Gregor's illness and relinquishing of his title. All of Angyra needs to see us married and united. Is that clear?"

"Quite," she said, her chin snapping up again. "Duty above all else. A public show of support when our marriage is based on the pretense that we are happy."

He inclined his head in a sharp decisive nod. "Angyra needs you, Demetria. *I* need you as well."

"Do you really?"

Dammit, he'd said too much. Let his emotions be bared for a heartbeat. "I need a Queen at my side. The people know you. Like you." Whereas they barely tolerated him.

She was his buffer. The means by which he hoped to gain favor with the people. He hated her because she was favored and he was not. But he wouldn't tell her that. He wouldn't give her that much power over him.

"How good that someone finds favor with me," she said, her tone peevish. "But I still insist on selecting the fabric for my gown, and I need it done as quickly as possible."

"Tell me what you want and I'll have it delivered to you."

She rolled her eyes, as if she found his suggestion foolish. "I need to select the fabric myself. Even the most fabulous design is nothing if not paired with the right cloth."

"I thought the gown was to be made of silk," he said.

"There are thousands of bolts of various types of silk. I can't tell which will be the perfect one until I touch it."

She strode into her bedroom and returned a moment later, with two garments on hangers and a length of cloth draped over her arm. A black blouse held a rich sheen, and a coral dress looked warm and alluring against her skin.

"These are made from silks I bought in Istanbul," she said,

holding each up. "They are ideal for the selected garment, but would be all wrong for the other."

"I will take your word for it," he said.

She huffed out a frustrated breath. "Perhaps this will convince you. Look at this fabric I bought." She held it up and gave the length a shake, causing a dark rainbow of colors to dance across the cloth. "Don't you see? When it moves, it looks alive."

What he saw was an independent woman who would delight in butting heads with him. A passionate woman who fired his blood. A woman who knew what she was talking about in regards to fabric and designs.

Kristo silently admired both traits, for he didn't want a meek wife, nor one who lacked passion. He wanted Demetria.

He wanted to see the desire she felt for her designs directed at him. He longed to nip at the lush fullness of her lips, tease the corners of her mouth before he trailed kisses down the slender column of her neck. Wanted her to moan and writhe against him in a silent plea to do more. Until she begged him to take her now.

But beyond sex he wanted this strong woman to embark on this royal journey by his side. Dammit, he wanted to trust this strong, passionate woman to be his partner in all things.

Yet how could he think of such a thing when she'd been unfaithful to his brother? When she would likely betray him, given the chance? When she was still keeping a secret from him?

Their gazes collided, and he grimaced as her silent entreaty arrowed straight into him. She proved her point well.

It was her design. It was her wedding gown. She should choose the fabric, not someone else.

"Very well. I'll have the plane made ready and inform Vasos we will be leaving the palace," he said. "We'll leave for Istanbul in the hour."

Her face lit up. "Thank you. It will only take me a moment to change."

She dropped the shimmering cloth on the sofa and hurried into the bedroom. In moments he heard the spray of water in the en suite bathroom.

It would be so easy to strip to his skin. To slip into the shower beside her. To take her.

He flexed his fingers. Drew in a deep breath, then another. Now wasn't the time to go to her, no matter now much he wanted her.

His gaze fell on the shimmering fabric. He fingered it and felt something clutch low in his gut. She was right. When it moved it looked alive.

If she wore a gown made from it no man would be able to tear his gaze from her. They would do anything to please her, to earn a rare brilliant smile.

Wasn't that what he'd just done?

With a muffled curse he swept from the room and stalked to his own. No woman had ever dared to stand up to him like that before. None had challenged him.

They fawned and demurred to his will—in bed and out of it. Their simpering disgusted him, for they were all shallow and selfish.

"Find a woman who is your equal, Kristo," his mother had told him.

Perhaps he had.

She was strong. Beautiful. Desirable.

And not to be trusted.

Above all else he must bear that in mind.

The flight to Istanbul seemed far shorter than the one that had brought Demetria to Angyra. On that trip fear had ridden her shoulders and throbbed in her belly. This time she brimmed with an odd mix of excitement and confusion.

She'd been resigned to her arranged marriage to Gregor, but this upcoming wedding to Kristo was too new. Too emotionally charged with anger and lust and hurt.

You could get out of it.

And she could.

She could refuse him at the altar.

Or, better yet, she could escape him today and get lost in the crowds. She could return to Athens and the career she'd dreamed of having.

But to do so would alienate herself from her family. It would create a scandal that would be far worse than the one her mother had caused so long ago.

That was not the reputation she wanted.

"Why the long face, *agapi mou*?" he asked, startling her from her troubled thoughts.

She waved a hand, as if trying to grab an answer out of thin air. She certainly couldn't divulge what had just gone through her mind!

Her gaze fixed on Vasos, who was busy speaking with one of the other guards, likely going over details once they landed.

"Do they always travel with you when you leave the palace?" she asked, her mind ticking off every moment she'd spent alone with Kristo. The times she'd *thought* they were alone. "Everywhere?"

He dipped his chin. "Vasos has been with me for years. Why do you ask?"

Heat rushed to her cheeks, for she knew now that even if the guard wasn't seen he was still nearby. Watching.

Vasos had shadowed Kristo around the globe. From the crush of casinos to the most celebrated ski lodges to those moments he'd needed to get away from it all. Like the beach?

"Why?" A near hysterical bark of laughter burst from her. "My God! That day on the beach. He was there, wasn't he? He

watched it all from some secluded vantage point and *you*—" she spat the word, sputtering with anger "—you let him!"

He was out of his chair and bending over her before she could blink. His dark eyes narrowed into dangerous slits, the irises flaring a warning glint that she'd gone too far.

"Get a grip on yourself," he said.

"How can I when he…? When you…?" She shook her head, too humiliated and angry to finish the troubling thought.

"You must think very little of me if you believe for one moment that I would let any man see you naked," he all but hissed. "I'd never make love with a woman in front of him. Never!"

"But you said he went everywhere with you."

"Within reason." He pushed away, looking down on her with open disgust. "Don't believe everything you've read about me."

Demi caught a note of hurt in his eyes before he slammed shut the door on his emotions. Just like that he shut her out, this time making her feel like a fool in the process.

And this time she deserved it!

She pressed her hot face in her hands, mortified that she'd overreacted so. It wasn't like her to behave so irrationally.

How cruel of her to insult him so when he'd granted her this concession regarding the creation of her wedding gown. When he'd gone to the trouble to take her to Istanbul as she'd asked.

"I'm sorry," she said, her voice as low as her spirits.

They'd done very little but argue and snip at one another. It was time to let the animosity go. Time to try and forge a new future together.

Unless she'd just ruined that one chance.

His heavy sigh echoed between them. "You are quite good at disparaging my name, even though you claim to know nothing about my tainted reputation."

"Then enlighten me," she said. "Talk to me about your wants. Your dreams. Your foibles and your triumphs. Let me get to know you."

His gaze bored into hers, then sliced quickly away. The break as clean and cold as the slash of a blade.

She blinked, hurt that he now stared at the window.

That his silence told her he was ignoring her.

She hated him for his ability to shut her out. To block off all emotion.

And yet for a moment, when their gazes met, she'd glimpsed a keen longing in him. A need that reached out to her. That touched her as nothing else ever had. Almost like a little boy lost.

That was surely a trick of the eye.

Clearly there was nothing soft or needy about Kristo Stanrakis. She'd thought him reminiscent of a pagan god from the sea that day at the beach and that hadn't changed. Nor had the urge to get close to him ebbed. But nothing hinted there was a caring man buried deep inside him.

Had the laughing, passionate man she'd frolicked with been nothing more than a chimera? Had she seen what she'd desperately wanted to see in him instead of the truth?

The answers eluded her, even after they'd landed and the two of them had embarked on this expedition to buy cloth for her wedding gown. Or rather the five of them, if she counted Vasos and the other two brawny guards.

"Do you know the address of this shop?" Kristo asked as he escorted her off the plane, his hand at her elbow firm and sending jolts of sensual awareness coursing through her.

"Yes."

She managed to give the address without stammering, though it was an effort. If he kissed her like he had that day, if he caressed her as she'd dreamed of him doing for a year, if he made love to her with the same intensity that blazed in his dark eyes then she'd be lost.

How could she be drawn to this man who clearly had no tender feelings for her? She didn't know. But keeping her distance from him was her only defense. And even that was a weak one.

She chafed her arms against the sudden chill of loneliness. Would she ever understand Kristo?

It seemed doubtful right now. Instead of growing closer, as she'd hoped, they seemed to be drifting further apart.

Until they reached the car. Then she was all too aware of him as a potent male, as their driver negotiated the congested streets with Vasos up front and the other two guards following in a separate car.

Every curve tossed her against Kristo's broad shoulder. Every breath she took pulled his essence deep into her soul.

Each brush of his thigh against hers served to remind her of them sprawled on a sun-warmed slab of stone with arms and legs tangled.

It seemed an eternity passed before they arrived at the draper's shop. She breathed a relieved sigh and put distance between her and Kristo, but that was short-lived as he kept a hand at her back when they entered the shop.

The congested room seemed more cramped with Kristo towering beside her.

"Ah, you have returned," the Turkish draper said. "What do you wish to have?"

"I'm looking for an ivory silk," she said.

He bobbed his shaggy head. "For dresses? Blouses, perhaps?"

"A wedding gown."

"Ah." The little man flicked a glance at Kristo and smiled. "I have two bolts that you might like."

He rushed into his back room, leaving her alone with Kristo. Of course he was still standing far too close.

She moved to the other side of the tiny shop on legs that trembled and examined the reels of lace on display. But it took several moments of steadying her breath before she could focus on the trims and nets instead of the man. Before she could even begin to imagine which ones she'd need for the gown.

"Do you come here often?" Kristo asked, coming no closer, and yet his rich voice wove around her just the same.

"I've been here a few times," she admitted as she selected a bolt of cream tissue veiling that matched a reel of fine silk lace.

The draper returned with two bolts of silk and her thoughts immediately focused on the fabric. They were spectacular. But only one swirled from the bolt like thick cream. Only one had that rare tactile blend of ethereal and sensual to the touch, making it perfect for her wedding gown.

"You like this one?" Kristo said, reaching across her to feel the fabulous ivory silk.

She nodded, reveling in that special thrill that always rippled through her when she found the right cloth. "It is the perfect texture and color. And see?" she said, running a finger down the weave end. "Nothing has been taken off this bolt yet."

"Then we will take all of it," Kristo said. "You do not want someone to duplicate your gown with the same fabric."

No, she didn't, and she'd been prepared to explain that to him. But he knew. Somehow he'd realized the importance of this fabric being exclusive to her gown, though there would surely be duplications made.

And again she felt that odd bond between them. Here and gone, but he did understand what this meant to her. He was ensuring that this at least remained special to her.

"Thank you." She turned to the draper and smiled. "This bolt and these trims, please."

The little man bobbed his head. "I will send to Athens?"

"No. I'll take this package with me today," she said.

"Vasos will see it's delivered to the plane." Kristo faced the draper. "The price?"

The Turkish supplier rattled off a staggering sum that she was prepared to haggle over. But Kristo tossed euros on the counter and took her arm.

She caught a glimpse of Vasos stepping out of the shadows to see to the cloth before Kristo escorted her out into the street. The market teemed with locals and tourists, and the air was redolent with spicy odors from the vendors.

"There is a restaurant two blocks over that is superb," Kristo said. "We can wait for Vasos and the car, which would be his preference, or walk the distance now."

So he did chafe at the constraints he had to live with. "Let's walk. It's a beautiful day." And on the street she would be spared being closeted with him a bit longer.

He bent to speak with their driver, then took her hand and started down the street. She wanted to resent his hold on her, to pull away from the long strong fingers entwining with hers.

She wanted to find revulsion in his touch instead of pleasure. Her insides quivered in anticipation of a closer intimacy even as her mind tried to rebel against such thoughts.

But the rightness that swept over her at just being with this man left her struggling to make sense of her own emotions. She didn't want to hate him. She wanted to know him. Love him.

But that would be foolish. Dangerous.

He didn't want her love. He wanted her body. She had to remember that. She had to look at this pragmatically.

Duty bound them together. The passion they shared made it bearable. No, more than that. Addictive.

It wasn't love. It never would be. But she had to think it was better than what she would have had with Gregor, for he clearly didn't even lust after her.

With Gregor, she'd forget what he looked like one year to the next. Not so with Kristo.

It had shamed her to admit she'd secretly desired him for a year. She'd grieved over how she could possibly marry one brother while she lusted for another.

But that didn't stop the wanting. She remembered every moment of them together on the beach.

His wind-tousled hair and the curl that stubbornly fell onto his strong brow. The feel of his muscles bunching beneath her hand. The heat of his body covering hers.

And his hands. God, how she would dream of those hands on her body, and some nights shamefully touch herself as he had and wish he was there.

"Be careful what you wish for," her father had told her.

Now that wish was true.

Now she would have Kristo. Or at least the small part of himself that he was willing to give her.

It wasn't enough, even though the sensations rocketing through her now were beyond anything she'd ever felt before. Stronger. More intense.

Surrendering to those feelings would only hurt her in the end. He'd take her. Make her his wife, his lover. But he'd never give her his heart. He'd never fully trust her.

She'd expected him to choose an elegant restaurant, but he led her to a small café with an excellent view of the sea and an old-world charm that embodied the glory of the Ottoman Empire. The owner greeted him as if he were a pasha, and quickly provided a secluded table for their dining pleasure apart from the crowd.

"The *mezzes* are delicious," he said.

She hadn't thought she was hungry, but the spicy smells wafting in the air awakened a hunger in her. She grasped it, for that was preferable to the hunger she felt for Kristo. This was one she could sate without feeling guilty.

"What would you like?" he asked.

"You decide," she said, and was rewarded with one of his rare smiles.

"*Mezzes* to start," he told the waiter. "Then the aubergine stuffed with grilled quail, with a bottle of your best Yeni Raki."

Her resolve began to melt. Was he trying to seduce her? Wine and dine her? Was that the reason for his sudden attention?

In moments the waiter returned with a bottle of wine. Before she could decline any, a glass was poured and set before her.

"A toast to finding the perfect fabric for your gown," Kristo said, raising his glass, his mesmerizing gaze daring her to refuse.

"To the most perfect silk in all of Istanbul." She clinked her glass against his and took a sip, just as a waitress bustled over with a tray laden with cheeses and stuffed vine leaves.

He selected one and lifted it to her mouth, his charming smile simply taking her breath away. No man had ever looked at her with such blatant passion. None had ever flirted with her so openly.

She didn't want his attention, for it held no meaning besides carnal pleasure for him. Yet she was powerless to refuse the offering either.

The café shrank to just the two of them, the air pulsing with hot spices and hotter desire. She opened her mouth, intending to take no more than a bite, but he expertly slipped the morsel past her lips, his fingertips brushing the fullness of her lower one in a move that made her insides clutch.

She trembled at the power in that slight caress. Sighed as the combination of the sour cherry-filled leaves exploded in her mouth, the delicacy more enticing because of his nearness.

"I will take great pleasure in seeing you stand beside me and exchange vows, *agapi mou*."

"Will you?" she asked, feeling suddenly breathless under the intensity of his gaze.

"Of course. Perhaps I should ask you that question."

Her pleasure faded, for that was the last thing she wanted. The truth would surely break this magical spell. Yet she couldn't ignore him either, so she settled on a truth that spared her personal feelings.

"Without a doubt you will be the most handsome groom Angyra has ever had," she said. "I'll be honored to stand beside you."

And she'd be the happiest woman on earth if he would come to care for her. If he'd one day trust her.

If only she hadn't succumbed to him that day on the beach they'd be starting this journey without this sense of betrayal between them. But, as he'd said before, what was done was done. They had to learn to live with their mistakes.

"Have you heard from Gregor?" she asked, aware that mentioning his name would raise that invisible barrier between them.

And it did.

His shoulders racked tight. His gaze grew remote. His features hardened with worry and something she couldn't name.

"No. I can only assume nothing has changed." He popped a sliced feta into his mouth and chewed, but she felt the distancing in him immediately. "Mikhael is with him and will call if—" His brows pulled into a troubled frown and a bleakness chilled his eyes. "If he takes a turn for the worse."

She reached across the table and rested her hand on his. To her surprise he turned his hand over and clasped hands with her.

The bond felt strong. Sure. Yet she knew it was a tenuous thing.

"This has been such a tragic time for your family," she said. "Your father had lived his life, but Gregor is still a young man."

He rocked back in his chair and studied her, breaking the physical connection but not the internal one that pulled at her heartstrings. "Tell me. What did you and my brother talk about when you were alone?"

"My duty as Queen. Gregor was quite honest with me. He promised that he'd treat me kindly, but said that I wasn't to expect a close relationship with him." She gave a wry laugh. "As for his own expectations—all he asked was that I honor my vows until I'd gifted him with heirs."

"A promise you broke before the wedding," Kristo said, but this time the accusation lacked that caustic bite.

Still she refused to look at him, to see the censure and hate that would surely blaze in his eyes. "To my shame."

"To mine as well," he said, surprising her. "You showed interest in the sea turtles, in what I was doing to protect them."

That brought her gaze up to his. "I thought it was a noble thing to do. I still do."

A smile tugged briefly at his mouth. "Then you are in the minority. My conservation work has not always met with approval from the people. Neither have all the safety measures and regulations I have implemented at the Chrysos Mine."

"I didn't know that you were involved in the mine," she said.

"Few people do—which is how I want it," he said. "My

duty to the crown was to serve as ambassador as well as guard our homeland's natural treasures. That includes the rare Rhoda gold that is only found on Angyra."

She stared at him, stunned to see this serious side of the man that he'd kept hidden. "Who has taken over those duties now that you are King?"

A sigh rumbled from him, and a shadow of concern passed over his features. "Mikhael will serve as ambassador, as well as become overseer at the mine. But I've yet to find someone who'll take an interest in conserving the sea turtles' nesting grounds."

"Can't you appoint a committee?"

"The thought has crossed my mind, but I'd prefer having an advocate in place."

"I could do it," she said. "You'd have to teach me—"

He held up a hand to silence her, looking far too regal and commanding for her peace of mind. "Out of the question."

"Why?"

"For one, the job requires intense coordination with the sea turtle conservation network. You could be gone days, weeks at a time." He took a drink of wine, his gaze intent on hers. "There can also be great danger involved. So even if such a position were possible for you, I'd not place you in harm's way."

"But—"

"There will be no more debate on this, Demetria."

They glared at each other across the table, both stubbornly refusing to bend. But Demi knew when she was fighting a losing battle, and really she didn't want to place herself in danger either.

She was in enough of that being with Kristo! So giving up this battle was easy to do.

There was enough animosity between her and Kristo already. She didn't need to go looking for more things that would drive them further apart. Still, she capitulated with a sharp lift of her chin to show she hadn't conceded easily.

"Surely you can convince someone in Angyra of the importance of safeguarding your natural treasures?" she said.

He shrugged, but she caught the pensive shadows in his eyes again and knew that this issue deeply troubled him. "I will not give up hope that someone will take over the task with the same energy as I have exhibited all these years."

And that was the crux of the matter. He was passionate about this, and a control freak as well. She almost pitied the person who'd take over the position, for Kristo would still find a way to oversee it.

How lucky the sea turtles were to have such a champion. What she wouldn't give if he'd devote that same attention to *her*!

An uneasy silence quivered between them. Kristo ate while she toyed with her food, her appetite waning again. As for her wine, she didn't remember drinking it all, but the slight buzz she felt told her she'd done so—and too quickly.

He refilled her glass and his own. "What of you and your half-sister? Are you close to each other?"

"We used to be when we were children," she said, glad for the change in topic, though she felt sad when she thought of her childhood. "After her mother became ill she leaned on me more. She needed my help, and protection from Father."

"Protection?" he repeated.

"Father has a horrid temper, and she tended to strain his patience," she said.

Something shifted in his features—not a softening, but a sharp change nonetheless. "Who was *your* protector, *agapi mou*?"

"I—I could take care of myself."

He bit out a curse. "You were a child."

She couldn't argue with that, but she had learned to do for

herself when she was very young for her stepmother had been too busy with a fussy baby and a husband who demanded all of her time. In fact she had very much been her stepmother's helper until that fateful day when the King of Angyra had paid them a visit.

"I was a child when the King of Angyra chose me to be the Crown Prince's bride," she said. The event was clear to her, for it was the catalyst that had changed everything at their house. "From then on I received special attention by way of a tutor."

She frowned, recalling too that her sister's demeanor had taken a decidedly petulant turn soon after. At the time she'd blamed the change on her stepmother's worsening health, and her death a year later. But had there been another reason?

Jealousy? It pained her to admit that her sister had inherited that trait from their father. That she was very much like him, which was why they constantly clashed.

"What aren't you telling me?" he asked, reaching across the small table again to stroke his fingers along her jaw. "What troubles you so?"

To her surprise, a swell of emotion lodged in her throat and brought sudden tears to her eyes. "I'm fine, really."

"No, you're not. Why the sad face, *agapi mou*? Are you pouting because I refuse to let you take over the task of conservationist?"

"Of course not," she said.

"Then what is it? What do you want?"

She knew better than confess what was in her heart. But as she stared into his dark eyes she felt a commiserating pang shoot from him to her.

He was the second son. The one passed over. Ignored. He must understand. He must feel this connection too.

"I want a husband who loves me," she whispered.

His sensuous mouth thinned, his hand dropping from her face. "That, I am afraid, is impossible."

A knife to the heart wouldn't have hurt as much.

CHAPTER FIVE

THE last thing Kristo wanted to deal with when he returned to Angyra late that afternoon was unrest at the Chrysos Mine. But the death of the King followed by the abdication of the Crown Prince had tended to leave the people feeling adrift. Abandoned. Wary of how effective a King he'd be.

The last was a worry that plagued him as well. The magnitude of his burden rested uneasily on his shoulders.

"Do not expect me to join you for dinner tonight," he told Demetria. "I have no idea when I'll return."

"That's all right. I'm still stuffed from our lunch in Istanbul."

He doubted that, for she'd eaten like a small bird, barely picking at her meal. But if she did grow hungry she had the palace kitchen at her disposal.

He turned to leave, but her words stopped him. "Thank you for today."

"It was my pleasure." And for the most part that was true. "Goodnight."

"Be careful," she said.

He only smiled, for nobody had ever charged him with that before. If he didn't know better he'd swear she cared about his welfare.

The uproar at the mine regarded the miners' concerns over who would be their new managerial overseer. All of them believed, as he and Gregor had intended from the start, that Gregor had been watching over their interests.

A select few knew he was the man responsible for seeing to their needs, and they kept silent as he'd hoped. But even if the truth had gotten out it was too late for anyone to believe he'd held this secretive role at the mine.

So he spent the evening listening to personal complaints and general worries. He took his time listening to each man. He didn't judge any matter as trivial.

By the time midnight rolled around he had the satisfaction of knowing the miners appreciated all he'd done for them. They also seemed relieved to know that Mikhael, who was a much-loved prince, would take over in his brother's stead.

Yet the greatest surprise was their reaction to Demetria. By and large the people loved her. And why wouldn't they?

She was young. Beautiful. Her effervescent smile lit up a room.

Most importantly, it was obvious that during her annual visits to Angyra she'd mingled with the people. She'd spoken with the Angyrans on their level. She'd gained their trust.

They saw her as one of them, soon to be elevated to the exalted role of Queen. Because of her impending marriage to him, they accepted Kristo as King. For now.

All in all it was enough to boost Kristo's much lagging ego as he made the trip back to the palace. Now if *he* could come to terms with his bride-to-be as easily...

He desired her. There was no denying that. But he would never trust her.

As for the love she sought...

It was unbelievable that she thought he could ever lose his heart to her—that she'd even want his affection.

Even if he had been prone to fall victim to such tender

emotions—which he most certainly was not!—he'd never fall in love with the woman who'd betrayed his brother.

His one concession—or was it in actuality a weakening toward her?—was allowing Demetria to design her wedding gown. That could have been a mistake. Not that she wasn't more than capable of designing a gown that would be much celebrated, that would rival any designer in the world, and would surely make him proud to have her on his arm!

No, the problem rested in that he feared she would continue to ask for more. If he wasn't watchful, she'd eat away at his defenses to gain more and more freedoms. Like her eagerness to take over the task of conservationist.

The very idea of her doing that boggled his mind. He suspected she'd put the same passion into that as she did everything else.

It would be like her to turn even that into a national holiday. He would not put it past her to create T-shirts for the schoolchildren to wear. Perhaps host a parade to celebrate the sea turtles returning to nest.

And she'd be away from the palace more than she was there.

If he were not watchful she'd likely usurp his role as King. Already she had the people's favor!

She tested his patience at every turn. Yet he wanted to make love with her so badly he physically ached.

In fact when he reached the palace it took effort to find his own apartment instead of hers. Even then, as he collapsed onto his bed in exhaustion, his last coherent thought was the pleasure he'd feel if she was lying in his arms.

Despite his short night, Kristo was up at six, savoring his coffee while he carefully checked the stock market online. It was a ritual he'd established long ago, when he'd been in the process of tripling his fortune. As it stood now, he was wealthier than any of his relatives—though he suspected Mikhael would rival him in that regard soon.

His concentration was broken when Vasos marched into his apartment, and by the look on the bodyguard's face he dreaded the news. "We have a problem."

"What now?" he asked, curious as to why Vasos had marched directly to the television and turned it on.

A leading celebrity gossip TV show out of Athens filled the screen. "Your upcoming marriage is this morning's top story."

"We've not hidden the fact that we are to marry in a little more than a week," Kristo said, having no interest in listening to the show's fanfare.

"Wait," Vasos said when he made to turn it off. "There is far more to the story than that."

Before Kristo could question his bodyguard, a picture of Demetria filled the screen. In the background was another image, one of an older man he didn't recognize.

"Our sources have discovered that there is much speculation regarding Demetria Andreou's birth," the immaculately garbed reporter said. "Less than a year before Demetria was born, her mother had a torrid affair with a noted Italian vintner."

Kristo stared in stunned silence as the reporter gave the highlights regarding Demetria's mother's story. Like Demetria, she'd been affianced to a wealthy Greek. And, like her daughter, she'd been unfaithful to her betrothal vows.

With a married man!

"The scandal has risen and ebbed over the years, though the last time it was briefly in the news was when Demetria Andreou was six years old," the reporter said. "That's when she was nicknamed 'scandal's daughter.' A cruel insult then, but now we've learned that the daughter has followed in her mother's footsteps. Only this time with royalty!"

No! This could not be happening.

"How could they know?" Kristo bit out, infuriated to hear a sensationalized version of his tryst on the beach with Demetria, of them betraying his brother. How they'd conspired to gain the crown together. "All lies! Who is responsible for this?"

Vasos pressed his thick lips together. "I've yet to discover the source."

"Keep at it. I want a name."

And he hoped to hell that name was Demetria Andreou!

He burst from his apartment and stormed down the hall to her suite, pushing open the door without bothering to knock. "Turn on your—"

The barked order withered on his tongue, for the TV was already on and the same reporter he'd listened to was wrapping up her shocking story. "We are sure there will be more breaking news out of Angyra soon. Stay tuned!"

"This is a nightmare," Demetria said, her complexion gray and her eyes wide with shock.

"It is far worse than that," he said, dreading what the repercussions would be on Angyra. "Who the hell did you tell about us?"

She clutched her head with both hands and sank onto the sofa, her face growing ghostly pale. "My sister. When I returned to the guesthouse that day she saw me and knew I'd been with a man. I tried to put off her questions, but she thought I'd been forced. She threatened to raise the guard. So I had to tell her the partial truth or she'd have caused an uproar."

And the truth would have come out then. In hindsight, that would have been preferable.

Kristo drove his fingers through his hair and swore. He'd

suspected someone close to Demetria had leaked this incident to the press, but he'd never guessed it would be her sister.

"Which she's done anyway, one year later." He planted his feet wide and glared at her. "Why would she do such a thing? Doesn't she realize the trouble this will cause you?"

"I suspect she's lashing out in anger because she won't be able to spend time at the show with me," she said, a dark flush staining her cheekbones. "Six months or more before the King died, I promised her that she could act as one of my models."

When she'd thought she'd have time before she would have to become Queen. But his father's death had slammed the door on those plans.

"She was upset when I told her I'd asked if you'd allow me this one show, but you'd refused."

He had. The very idea was preposterous.

"Your sister should realize that it was not your decision to make," he said. "Why bring this humiliation and shame down on you now? What did she hope to gain?"

"I doubt she thought that through," she said. "She's angry to have lost the chance to model and so she's sought to make me suffer as well."

"Suffer is putting it mildly." He paced before the cold hearth, outraged that her sister had brought this shame down on them, furious that Demetria had yet to show her own anger at her sibling. "Your sister has insulted the future Queen of Angyra. She's insulted the King!"

She flinched and turned a frightful shade of white. "As I said before, I am sure she never considered the repercussions."

He was not so sure. This act had taken malice and forethought. The revelation came when he desperately needed his kingdom to see him and Demetria as responsible leaders. Not two oversexed young people who'd betrayed the favored Crown Prince.

He muttered a dark curse. "I can't begin to imagine the trouble this will heap on us."

Her head bent and her slender shoulders bowed. "I'm so sorry. I vowed not to follow in my mother's footsteps," she said. "Yet I failed."

Seeing her looking defeated tore at his resolve to remain unmoved. He hated that she was getting to him again. But he hated it more that she was ready to shoulder this all alone.

"No! Your sister failed you." He dropped on the sofa beside her and drew her close, cursing silently when he felt a tremor shoot through her. "The scandal surrounding your mother—I need to know the whole story."

A weary sighed escaped her, and she collapsed a bit more against him. "Bear in mind that I only know what Father told me, for my mother died giving birth to me."

"I didn't know that."

Hell, he knew very little about this woman he was to marry other than her father was a greedy man. He hadn't even been aware that her sister was a half-sibling. Hadn't known that she had sought a career. Hadn't been aware she'd been her sister's protector—the mother figure that her sister had now clearly abused.

One year ago he hadn't even known what Demetria looked like now that she was an adult. He hadn't been curious about her.

Which made this particular drama today all the more vexing, for if he'd known about Demetria none of this would have happened.

But all he'd known was that she was the daughter of Sandros Andreou, a man he disliked for his shady business practices, and his first wife, a Greek nobleman's daughter who'd gotten embroiled in a scandal with a married man. Learning that she was their daughter had made it easier to think the worst of her.

Yet right now he was finding it impossible to blast her with the anger that boiled and seethed inside him. Dammit, he wanted to comfort her—for it was obvious that she was suffering over her sister's duplicity far more than he.

"Please. Go on with your story," he said, when the silence became too much to bear.

Again a sigh. A hesitation that told him she wasn't comfortable disclosing all. "According to my father, Mother fell madly in love with a suave Italian she met one summer. They had an affair, and my mother was certain marriage would follow."

"If the reporter was right, the man was already married with a family," Kristo said. "And your mother was unfaithful as well, for she was affianced to another man."

The irony of her daughter repeating history staggered him. But the fact that her sister had blabbed about his tryst with Demetria to the world infuriated him. It was an infraction he couldn't let go of.

"She was crushed when she learned the truth, and went into hiding at her father's house," she said. "But instead of her shame and humiliation fading into history, the story turned into a scandal when her lover's wife reported the story in retaliation. My mother's fiancé called off the wedding, and my maternal grandfather quickly arranged my mother's marriage to my father."

He imagined the old Greek had been well paid to take the scandalous daughter off his hands. Andreou would do anything for money.

"So now you have, in a manner of speaking, repeated history?"

"Yes." She stared at her clasped hands, still seeming only sorrowful instead of angry as was her due. "I was told the story faded until my mother died, nine months after that, and it was briefly in the news again when I was six."

"Why then?" he asked.

She shook her head. "I don't know, but it was a horrible time for me. That's when I was nicknamed 'scandal's daughter' at school. I didn't want to go, but Father made me. He said it would make me stronger, though I certainly didn't feel strong at the time!" She flushed and looked away. "But of course you must have known all of this."

"No, none of it." But hearing it now touched him deeply.

It had taken courage for her to deal with the scandal at such a tender age. Her mother's jaded past was her Achilles' heel.

His as well now. She was his woman. Would be his Queen.

And now they would have to deal with a scandal that could rock Angyra. It wouldn't have been such an issue for Gregor for he was the favored son. Not so for Kristo.

"What does this mean for us?" she asked.

"It is difficult to tell at this point, but it will likely not be good."

He pushed to his feet and crossed to the open French doors. The breeze washed over him but failed to cool his temper.

Below, the town was coming fully awake. The news of this would spread through every house like a summer storm. The question remained what damage it would leave in its wake.

"Your sister will regret causing this uproar," he said.

"You can't mean to seek vengeance against her." She stepped to the rail and stood just out of arm's reach, but he felt her gaze bore into him, felt her silently imploring him.

He refused to look at her. But the very ends of her long dark hair lifted and moved with the wind, as if alive and dancing down her slender back, as if trying to get his attention. Her exotic jasmine scent ribboned around him like ethereal scarves and beckoned him closer.

Not that he needed any urging.

It was his own personal challenge to resist her—holding himself back, not giving her the benefit of knowing he was wildly attracted to her even though her sister's interference could cause him untold grief. Even though he was furious with her sibling.

"Kristo?" she said, laying a tentative hand on his arm. "*Please*. You can't mean to seek revenge on my sister."

He jolted as if hit with lightning, when it was only that damned bolt of lust that he'd yet to overcome. But he would find a way to tamp it down. To control it instead of it controlling him.

"That is exactly what I intend to do," he said, his voice as dark as his mood.

"I can't let you hurt my sister," she said.

"I don't intend to hurt her," he said. "It is your father's responsibility to see that she atones for this fiasco she's brought upon us. I assure you that when Sandros Andreou realizes that his benefits as the father of my Queen could be jeopardized he will seek retribution himself."

Her hand slipped from his arm, and a cool distance yawned between them. Good! He couldn't think straight when she was hanging on him. Never mind that she'd barely pressed a hand to his. It had felt as if she was clinging.

"Please," she implored again, stubbornly defending her sister. "Don't you see? She's young and troubled. She does these things just to gain attention."

He whirled on her then, and grabbed her upper arms, dragging her so close he could see the flicker of uncertainty dance in her eyes. "I am not sure if you suffer from blind devotion to your family, or if you are so used to catering to her whims that you automatically rush to her defense even when it isn't warranted."

"I was the only one she could turn to when she was little," she said.

"But she's no longer a child. She has chosen a malicious way to strike back at you."

She looked up at him with pleading eyes. "Please. Just wait a bit before you contact my father. Let me talk to her."

He ground his teeth, furious with her. Demetria *was* blind to her sister's machinations. Her loyalty rested with someone who didn't deserve her concern. A woman she still saw as a child she needed to protect.

It was clear to him that her sister had exploited that nurturing trait in Demetria. That her sibling was as conniving as Andreou—a man who fed on greed.

But how the hell could he make Demetria see her sister for what she was? What did he have to do to make her open her eyes to the truth?

"Enough talk. I will handle this my way."

He strode to the door. He would not tolerate this slur on Demetria, for any insult to her was to him as well. And to Angyra!

But he'd barely made it halfway across the room before she launched herself after him.

"No," she said, slamming her back against the closed door. "Kristo, give this more thought."

Was she mad? "There is nothing more to think about. Now, move," he said, in no mood to haggle with her any longer.

"No! I am not letting you walk out of here when you are in this black mood."

Did she actually think that she could stop him? "You have no idea just how dark my mood could become if we continue to stand here arguing about your sister's interference in our lives when the answer is perfectly clear to me."

But instead of being sane and getting out of his way she raised her chin in defiance. "I can't let you do this."

That was not the thing to say to him. "You can't stop me."

He yanked her flush against his chest in a move that was

meant to intimidate. To put her in her place. To put an end to this ridiculous standoff.

Except the moment they touched, a different fury exploded within him, with all the raw force of a summer storm. He certainly wasn't a stranger to the pull of desire, but he hadn't experienced anything this powerful since that day with her on the beach.

And that was another sore spot, for since then he had yet to meet another woman who moved him so, who was gripped with the same passions as he. She popped into his thoughts at the oddest times, and haunted his dreams.

She was never to be trusted, yet the thought of her in his brother's arms had enraged him. Except now she was in his arms. Now she was his.

There was no reason to keep her at arm's length any longer. He wanted her. He'd have her.

He ripped out a rough growl and tightened his hold on her. The throb of her own desire pulsed through him.

"No," she breathed, eyes huge, shadowed with a clear understanding of just what erotically dangerous emotion she'd awakened by baiting him.

"Yes," he rasped, on fire for her.

A heartbeat later his mouth claimed hers in a kiss that was long and lusty and sizzling with all the emotions he'd held in check.

Always he held back with women.

Except with her.

She drew the best and worst out in him. God help them, for they would surely drown together in a maelstrom of passion.

He pulled back once to drag air into his starving lungs. For a charged moment the haze of passion cleared and sanity flickered before him.

Her fists pressed against the wall of his chest but her

resistance had ebbed. The wide eyes that had pleaded with him were now clouded with a mixture of passion and confusion.

He should leave now, while he could. He shouldn't take her when his emotions were this wild and troubled.

And perhaps he would have left if that tiny sound of need hadn't escaped her parted lips. If her fingers hadn't uncurled from those tight fists and splayed on his chest.

One strap had slid down her arm, baring skin that was as smooth as cream. At that moment she looked like a Grecian goddess come to life. Diana, perhaps. Or Persephone.

Or Venus?

Reason went up in flames.

He hissed out a breath of raw need. He'd sooner stop breathing than leave her now, when all he could think about was running his fingers down the slender slope of her neck, down to the heaving rise of her bosom, across the nipples that had pebbled against the delicate cloth of her dress.

Dammit, he needed her. He'd have her now!

He wanted his mouth to adore her body again. To kiss every inch of her smooth skin. To savor her taste and texture until she screamed his name. Until she begged him to take her.

He dipped his head and captured her mouth, unleashing a side of him that he'd kept reined in. The moment his lips molded to hers the heat of her passion sent his last coherent thought up in flames.

A shiver ripped through her. Her fingers dug into his shoulders, clinging almost desperately.

Her lips moved against his with the same desperate hunger, on and on, until they were both lightheaded and gasping for breath.

They broke apart slightly to draw in air, foreheads pressed together and breaths sawing hard and fast. Her fingers wadded his shirt, the nails grazing his skin to stoke the fire deep in him, her breath hot on his neck.

If he'd set out to put her in her place, to show her who was the ruler in this, he'd surely failed—for it was clear to him at this moment that her place was right here in his arms. He didn't want to dominate her now. Just to make love with her.

"This would be the ideal time to stop, before this goes too far," he said, surprised his voice remained steady, with his blood roaring in his ears and his skin so tight and hot he thought he'd split in two.

"It would," she said, nipping his lower lip. "But why should we?"

CHAPTER SIX

HE RAN the pad of his thumb over her lips and a sensual energy uncurled within her, leaving her trembling and leaning into his touch. She stared into his dark eyes and felt as if she were drowning in passion so intense that it sapped the strength from her limbs.

Since the day they'd met on the beach he'd invaded her thoughts as surely as his ancestors had invaded this island and claimed it for themselves.

There was certainly nothing to gain by saving themselves for their wedding night. In fact it would be wiser to sate their passions now, for then she wouldn't have that expectation later. She wouldn't be tempted to think how that special night *should* be between newlyweds.

His scent, his kiss, was already branded on her memory— the yardstick by which she'd unconsciously judged other men. Men who should have counted, who should have captured her heart—instead of this dark prince she'd fallen madly, passionately in love with.

Not his brother, the man she'd been destined to marry. But Kristo. Always Kristo invaded her dreams.

It was time to face her future. Face the truth she'd ignored for a year.

Kristo Stanrakis was an addiction she couldn't shake. He

had captured her interest long ago. Now he held her fate in his oh-so-strong hands.

All she was to him was an arranged wife with the correct lineage. The means to an end.

Yet that still didn't stop the yearning that plagued her. It didn't lessen the desire that coursed through her—desire he set ablaze with one heated look.

"You are mine," he said, sliding his palms down her sides and setting off a seismic tremor inside her.

His arrogance should disgust her. Instead she heard herself saying, "That goes both ways, Kristo!"

"Vixen," he said, before his lips captured hers.

Her resistance popped like a soap bubble as the flames of desire licked over her. She clung to him, desperate to know what it felt like to dance this close to the sun again.

She wanted to see if the reality of finally making love with this man came close to the teasing memory of hot kisses and intimate caresses that had haunted her for a year. She wanted to fill this awful emptiness inside her.

Their lips met in a collision of scorching need. The flames of desire danced around her and her skin pebbled, burning for him.

His hands were all over her, pushing up her shirt. He was tearing himself from her while he whipped it over her head. He pulled her up against him a breath later, and the crush of bared breasts to hot muscular chest surely set off sparks in the room. Her nipples budded and burned, and heat arrowed straight to her heart to explode in a burst of color.

No, this was far more intense than that day on the beach. This was cataclysmic. Primitive. Greedy.

His mouth fused on hers in a deep hot lick of desire that made her toes curl and her heart thrum with need. She dragged her nails down his sides to find the fastenings on his trousers.

She'd never been bold with a man, but he brought that out in her as well. Slowly she undid his trousers, her knuckles riding along the hot length of his sex.

A low growling sound came from him, the vibration singing along her nerves. She felt power flow into her limbs, felt the rightness of being with him pulse in her veins.

Still it wasn't enough. She glided her hands down his hot muscular body, her open mouth following the lazy path, tasting salt and spice and finding it a powerful aphrodisiac.

He muttered a torrent of Greek, his voice no more than a rumble of sound. The heat and length of his sex branded her belly when she longed to have him in her.

She heard the button at her waistband pop. Shivered as the pad of his thumb rode the zipper down her side. Then her skirt and her panties were gone.

It went wild after that. As primitive as that day on the beach. Only this time nothing was holding them back. Nothing stopped them from taking this to the limit and beyond.

Their hands were all over each other, tossing embers on a fire that was already burning out of control. They strained against each other in a fluid rhythm that was timeless, mouths feasting on each other in wild abandon, tongues dueling in hot promise of what was to come.

She was dimly aware of him sweeping her up in his arms, of feeling a tremor streak through him. Of feeling the evidence of his desire against her hip.

She gasped as the sharp thrum of carnal need throbbed through her, breathing in his spicy scent and feeling drugged by his power. Feeling free to love him.

Then he was pressing her down on the bed, covering her with his length, and her thoughts blurred. She hooked a hand behind his neck to bring his face down to hers, to hold on to him like a lifeline, for she was spiraling out of control and needed him to ground her.

He obliged with a soft curse, his mouth fixing on hers as he drove into her in one long shuddering thrust. Finally, she thought. And it was beyond what she'd imagined.

Her back bowed on one long trembling gasp as she felt him tremble over her. In her. The connection was electric. Perfect.

"No..." he breathed, going still as death as his glazed eyes bored into hers. "You can't be a virgin."

His arrogantly handsome face looked so stricken, so stunned by that realization, that she slipped her arms around his broad shoulders in a gesture of comfort. He'd believed the worst of her, and in truth she had warranted a good deal of his anger.

She could only hope that he realized now that the incident on the beach with him had been her only indiscretion. That she'd been helpless to refuse him then. Or now.

"I'm not anymore," she said, her fingernails grazing the strong column of his neck.

Some emotion she couldn't imagine flickered in his eyes. Something she didn't understand. That touched her heart as nothing else had.

"A virgin," he said, sounding surprised it was so. That he was the only man she'd known this way. "Mine," he repeated, before his mouth fused on hers in a deep languid kiss that simply drove all other thoughts from her mind.

Then he moved in her. Fast. Hard.

Their lovemaking wasn't refined, but that was the last thing she wanted.

Each hard deep thrust lifted her higher, toward the promise of an explosive climax. The world narrowed to just them. Just sex with the one man she'd never been able to deny.

Yet it was more than that too. It was as if she'd waited a lifetime for this moment. This man.

Don't think like that. But the thought stuck. The fairy-tale wish. A dream to hang on to when she knew—*knew!*—that this wasn't love.

Just when she thought she'd die with need, he pushed her into that blindingly sensual place she'd heard about. This was beyond compare, beyond words.

She dug her fingers into his hot sweaty shoulders and hung on, flying into the mists of an explosive climax and wondering if she would simply get lost in this ethereal wonder of sensations. If she'd ever come back to earth. To him.

As if he knew she was drifting from him, he banded his arms around her as he thrust into her once more, holding her tight, binding her to him. She felt his entire body jerk and quake a heartbeat before she was lost to passion yet again. She could no longer think, just surrender to the sensations tearing through her in hot rippling waves.

Afterward she lay in the cocoon of his embrace, his big body covering hers, his face pressed beside her own. She drank in the moment with short frantic breaths, her heart still beating too fast.

She'd never experienced anything remotely close to this before. Never dreamed anything this powerful could touch her.

"Why didn't you tell me you were an innocent?" he rasped, clutching her close to him, staring at her with an intensity that robbed her of breath.

"Would you have believed me if I had?"

The beautifully sculpted bow of his lips thinned. "No. Probably not at the time. Only when we did make love, when I realized how incredibly tight you were, would I have allowed such a thing was possible."

He still wouldn't have believed her word for it. He'd needed proof.

Well, now he had it—though he didn't seem pleased at the discovery. What a contradictory man!

"It hardly matters now," she said, hoping to put an end to this conversation.

He stared at her, his classically smooth Greek brow furrowing deeply. "How can you say that?"

She wasn't at all surprised that he was agonizing over this. He didn't like to be wrong, and she'd just shattered his perception of her. "Because it's true. We are betrothed."

"We weren't that day on the beach!"

Their arguments always came back to this. As usual, she couldn't say anything but the truth in her defense. She'd never given a man such liberties before. She simply hadn't been able to resist him.

Brittle silence crackled and sizzled between them.

He rolled to his feet, clearly not the least bit shy about prowling the room gloriously naked. And it certainly was much more enjoyable to admire his beautiful body than meet that handsome face when he was angry.

"Do you realize the disaster it would have caused if I'd taken your virginity then?" he asked.

"Yes! I couldn't have lived with myself," she admitted, pulling the sheet over her body, for unlike him she was not comfortable flaunting her nudity, especially when they were in the throes of an argument. "As it was I agonized over how I could possibly attend any family function with you present. How I could be in the same room with you and not be tormented with memories of lying in your arms."

The last seemed to have gotten through to him, for he stopped pacing and just stared at her. Finally he gave a crisp nod. "I was plagued with much the same thoughts in coping with my betrayal as well."

And that, she realized with a sense of sadness, would never change. Neither of them had fought that initial attraction that had surged between them with the force of a tsunami. They'd surrendered to passion.

If the church bells hadn't tolled and broken through that drugging haze of desire she would have given him her virginity that day.

"So what now? Do we keep arguing the same point?" she asked. "Do we let it shroud what we've shared?"

She saw the struggle going on inside him—the deep pulling of his brow, the narrowing of his eyes, the tense bunching of incredibly beautiful male muscles. And her heart ached for this proud, loyal man.

"No," he bit out at last. "But I can't forget the past either."

"Of course not. Please… Let's go forward, because what we just shared was—" Near perfect? A moment she'd cherish all her life?

He returned to the bed and gathered her in his arms, the intensity of his expression shifting from anger to passion. "Go on. Say it. What was it to you, Demetria?"

She stroked the strong line of his jaw and smiled. "Wondrous. I didn't know such pleasure was possible."

"That was just the beginning, *agapi mou*."

His mouth captured hers in a long lingering kiss that had her blood humming with pleasure. In moments she was lost in his arms, his passion.

And for now it was enough.

It was inconceivable that she had been a virgin!

After making love again—this time slowly, tenderly—Demetria had curled against his side and surrendered to sleep. Her right hand rested on his chest, over his heart. Her breath was warm on the skin.

For the first time in his life he didn't wish to leave a woman's bed. He didn't want to be the one to break this connection that he simply had no words for.

Beyond the guilt that plagued him was the pleasure he'd

gained from knowing that Demetria was his and his alone. He was the first man she'd made love with. He'd be her last!

But, as much as he'd enjoyed this interlude with her, and as much as he dreaded to leave their bed, duty called him.

The Royal House of Stanrakis had been struck with scandal before, but never had brother been pitted against brother. Never had a woman come between them—a woman who'd be their Queen.

This latest slur on their names had to be dealt with swiftly. He grabbed his mobile off the bedside table and rang Sandros Andreou.

Kristo made his displeasure clear to the old Greek in a minimum of words. In turn Andreou assured him that he'd deal with his daughter.

With that matter settled, Kristo focused on the larger issues. The probable loss of loyalty among the people of Angyra was another matter entirely, and one that the State Council and the royal lawyers needed to review.

One mistake could cost him the support of those in powerful positions. His popularity among the people was already tenuous. But the high esteem the people held for Demetria would surely dim as well, so he couldn't rely on her to make him more favorable.

The only thing in their favor was that he was certain her sister had no proof of what had happened between him and Demetria on the beach. It was just speculation. Gossip.

He and Demetria simply had to convince the people that this was a vicious attack on the crown. That their day on the beach had been spent observing the sea turtles instead of almost making love.

That he hadn't been the irresponsible playboy prince who cared nothing for his country. That Demetria shared his passion of protecting Angyra's resources.

Passion. They certainly were well suited in that regard.

He toyed with a strand of her dark hair and allowed a grim smile. They'd set a pattern of anger melding into passion that knew no bounds. But this time when they came together it had been a firestorm of desire.

She possessed the ability to storm past his defenses as well as fuel his anger.

And he *was* angry.

At her. At himself for losing sight of his objective and taking her like a rutting young buck.

But it was an experience he'd cherish as well. He'd felt the burn clear to his soul and he wanted more. He knew if he kissed her, stroked her, she'd come alive in his arms again.

His mouth went dry, for though the bedsheet covered her, the image of her womanly curves was branded on his memory. His goddess in the flesh.

Before he could stretch out beside her and fully explore that possibility his mobile rang. He muttered a curse as he grabbed the object of intrusion off the bedside table.

The call he'd been expecting was right to the point. The council and the lawyers would meet with him in one hour in the Royal Statehouse.

He rolled from the bed and threw on his clothes, painfully aware of how delicate this situation was. He wanted it taken care of now, for the sooner they quelled this vicious gossip the better Gregor would be able to cope with it when it reached him—if it hadn't already!

"What's wrong?" she asked.

"The council is convening in an hour."

She rolled off the other side of the bed and gathered the sheet in her wake. The sight of her took his breath away, for she was the image of a Grecian goddess. Pure. Untouchable. The object of all men's desires.

He glanced at his Cartier watch and grimaced. "I must leave now."

"Fine. I'll deal with my sister—"

"I have taken care of that problem."

Her mouth dropped open. "What? How?"

"She is your father's responsibility," he said, and she stiffened as if he'd slapped her. "Finish your gown, *glyka mou*. Stay in the palace—for the people could raise an uproar when the scandal breaks."

"How touching that you are concerned about me," she said.

He set his teeth. She continued to bait him on this. "It is my duty to safeguard you and the heir that you may be carrying."

The color drained from her face. It was clear she hadn't considered that possibility.

But he certainly had after he'd made love with her spontaneously without protection. After he'd realized he was her first lover. When he'd made love to her again and again with the hope of planting his seed in her.

She was his—now and forever.

Hopefully the State Council and the lawyers would reach a swift decision today. He looked forward to returning to her. To making love with her.

He rounded the bed and strode toward her. To his surprise she held her ground. "When I return from this meeting we will face the people together, *agapi mou*."

"Will you stop calling me that?" she said, her voice breaking on a quiver. "I'm not your darling."

He stroked a finger along her jaw, smiling when a telltale moan escaped her softly parted lips. "Perhaps you are."

She stared at him, her breath coming too fast. Once again he was reminded that she wasn't experienced, as he'd assumed.

In that he'd judged her wrongly, but then when they'd first met she'd behaved shamelessly. Her passion had been open. Free. Just as it had been this morning.

"As I told you before, we can make ourselves miserable in this marriage or comfortable. But, no matter what, in public we will always appear happy. Understood?"

She gave a stiff nod. "As you wish, *Your Majesty.*"

He dropped his hand from the smooth curve of her jaw, his own hardening. She held such resentment over the simplest rules and orders. Perhaps when she was with child she'd mellow. Perhaps then she'd realize the magnitude of her duty.

"Rest while you can, Demetria."

For when they'd found a way to extinguish the heat of this scandal he intended to light a fire in her. They'd burn in the throes of passion together.

Demetria watched Kristo cross to the bedroom door, his stride assured and fluid. But through his thin shirt she saw the slabs of muscles in his back bunch and ripple with tension.

He wasn't as confident as he pretended to be.

Though he'd taken it upon himself to place demands on her father, this meeting with the council was an entirely different thing. She knew it, and she was worried about how it would turn out, how he would cope with whatever decision was agreed upon.

He was such a conflicted man!

When they'd made love, he had still been the same Kristo she'd met on the beach. Tall, strong and wildly protective of his domain.

Few people understood the significance of his work. Fewer still understood him.

She'd found his inner passion, and though she'd thought it would be trivial his quest touched her deeply.

Yet that didn't solve the greater issue that would always keep them apart. Her betrayal of his brother. His dying brother.

She wished that fate hadn't so cruelly brought them together like this. That they could have begun as friends instead of adversaries. That they were just two people without duty or a sordid past to tie them together.

"Please let me know what is happening," she said. "Don't keep me in the dark."

He stopped, back straight, one hand gripping the door. "Very well."

And then he was gone, his footsteps fading as he crossed the apartment. The door opened and closed with a decisive click.

She stood draped in a bedsheet and felt the ache of loneliness. Of rejection. Of confusion.

She'd thought the worst of him for so long. She'd believed that he was as shiftless and irresponsible as the tabloids painted him to be.

But that wasn't so. He was honorable. Proud.

He cared deeply for Angyra.

If only he cared for her as well.

CHAPTER SEVEN

MORNING came and went, with Vasos delivering a tray of *bougatsa* and steaming *elliniko café*. But, though she savored every drop of the thick Greek coffee, she took no more than a few bites of the scrumptious pastry oozing with rich cream cheese.

Her thoughts had ping-ponged between the scandal that her sister had stirred and erotic images of Kristo taking her in his arms and making slow sweet love to her.

For the first time she understood how he felt toward her, for he was tormented over betraying his sibling while she was the one feeling the sting of that very same thing from her sister. It was a cruel blow to have family deceive you.

And it was equally torturous waiting for word.

She had no idea how the royal lawyers and the council would view this ordeal. Would they deem Kristo unfit? Because her sister could not be circumspect, would they rescind her betrothal contract?

She went still at that possibility. If the council blamed her for this indiscretion, Kristo could set her free.

She could return to Athens, humiliated yet free. She could take part in the upcoming show. She could follow her dream to be a designer and have her heart's desire yet.

Except her heart's desire no longer held the same allure.

But Kristo did.

And what did that say about her? That she was a slave to passion? It was an admission that came hard, but it was her only excuse.

She certainly shouldn't love him. He was far too complicated. Far too arrogant.

No, she would marry for duty, just as she'd promised long ago.

If the council decided the wedding should proceed, the dress would be her swan song in the fashion world. A creation of hers that would be copied. Envied. That would leave no doubt that she could have been a driving force in haute couture.

If the wedding went through.

She bit her lower lip and wandered aimlessly around her apartment. Her future was up to the council and the royal lawyers. Along with Kristo, they'd decide whether to go on with the wedding. With her.

She couldn't imagine them turning on Kristo. He was their King. Even though he'd erred as well, it was as he'd said.

She'd betrayed the Crown Prince. She'd turned a blind eye to her betrothal vows.

No, they'd not turn their backs on royal blood. But she was a different matter entirely. She was simply the chosen bride for a King. The woman who might be carrying the royal heir now—and wouldn't that be ironic if she was banned from the kingdom?

She crossed to the wedding gown. Ivory silk draped over the form in the beginnings of her creation.

This was her dream gown, the one that was uniquely her.

But this wasn't her dream wedding.

Before her betrothal she'd imagined meeting one special man. Falling in love. Of wearing this gown on her wedding day and seeing appreciation and desire flare in her groom's eyes.

But she wouldn't have had that with Gregor. And all she'd ever have with Kristo was red-hot passion.

The wedding gown that would be her signature creation would symbolize a loveless marriage for the rest of her days. Bound to the one man who made her thrill to his touch, who made her want him even when she was furious with him!

She moved to the window and stared out at the water glittering like diamonds. What was taking the council so long to decide?

Demetria pressed her hands to her head and let out a frustrated groan. If she didn't busy herself she'd surely lose her mind just waiting. She turned back to the dress form and the temptation of finishing this gorgeous gown.

Soon she lost herself in work, and didn't stop until Vasos returned midday with a tray bearing lunch. "Do you require anything else?"

"No. But have you heard from the King?"

Vasos shook his head. "He is still in session with the council and the royal lawyers."

That didn't bode well for her or Kristo.

"If you don't need anything...?"

"I'm fine." Which was a lie. She was a bundle of nerves.

With a slight bow, he left the room.

She threw herself back into work. Whether she was deemed worthy to be the Queen or not, she had to complete the gown.

She was creating a masterpiece with every tuck, every ruching of silk, every cut, that would make the royal bride stand out from all other nobility.

She would be a vision to behold, the envy of all women. Nobody would know the angst roiling within her. How each stitch she'd made was bittersweet, for this gown should have symbolized her love for her husband.

By the time dusk fell her back ached and her fingertips

were sore. But, except for adding embellishments, the royal wedding gown was finished.

She stretched her arms overhead and moaned, her body protesting at the long hours of work on the heels of the passionate interlude she'd shared with Kristo. *Kristo.* Eight hours had passed and still no word from him.

She walked to the chaise and curled up, her mind plagued with worry while her body simply craved a moment's rest. This was by far the most tedious day of her life. How much longer would she have to wait before she knew her fate?

Kristo slipped into Demetria's suite just as night fully settled over Angyra. She'd been in his thoughts all day, but the need to see her had intensified the second the gruelling meeting with the council ended.

Now the fire of anger from that confrontation was doused as he stared down at Demetria's sleeping form. Her feet were bare, the toenails painted a shocking pink.

A gold chain encircled one slender ankle, and a small gold heart rested against skin that would be warm and smooth to his questing hands and mouth.

The delicate ankle bracelet wasn't an expensive piece of jewelry, yet on her it looked elegant. Classy.

His gaze lifted to the gown artfully arranged on the dress form. The design was simple, and as yet lacked the beading she'd depicted in her sketch. But the classic shape and clean lines screamed sophistication.

He could only imagine the breathtaking image she'd present, with the priceless crown jewels set in rare Rhoda gold lying against her light olive skin. How the large pearl pendant would rest between her full breasts, complementing the luminescent quality of the ivory silk.

She would be absolutely stunning in her wedding attire.

And positively breathtaking wearing nothing but the jewels on her wedding night.

A rueful smile tugged at his mouth. He readily admitted the desire she stoked in him, but he was loath to own up to those other sensations that were too new to examine closely. That he simply couldn't trust yet.

He stared down at the woman who would soon be his Queen. His wife. The mother of his children.

She looked small and vulnerable, yet sexy in a very earthy way. And exhausted.

He tipped his head back and heaved a sigh. He'd come straight here to break the news to her, but he hated to disturb her sleep now. When her father made good his threat she'd have enough sleepless nights ahead of her.

He turned to leave, though he ached to gather her close, to kiss her, thrust into her and narrow their world to just them. Just now.

"Kristo?"

Her voice reached out to him on a velvet echo, stroking his senses like a caress, pulling him back to her and the longings he couldn't deny.

He wanted to strip her bare and take her right here and now, on the narrow chaise that was ill-suited for all the desire pent up inside him. He was desperate to ease this longing that throbbed hot and heavy within him.

"I'm sorry I woke you," he said, still thinking to be noble, to walk out and leave her to her dreams if just for a few more hours.

"Don't be. How was the meeting with the council?"

"Hellish." He turned to face her, seeing no reason to delay telling her now.

She sat up, and one strap of her fuchsia tank top slid down her arm. The neckline drooped to reveal the smooth upper globes of breasts that were full and firm.

He ached to reach out and tug her top down a bit more to expose her bosom. To glide his fingers over every inch of her silken skin, then let his mouth follow the same path.

"Kristo, you're scaring me," she said. "What was decided?"

That he'd acted irresponsibly. That he was as much to blame as her, for if he'd been in attendance the preceding years when she'd visited, as had been expected of him, then he and Demetria would have known each other.

This dishonor would have been avoided.

"As we feared, every tabloid and gossip magazine has made us front-page news." He grimaced, for he'd had the displeasure of reading every one, all of which basically recounted the same story with a collage of snapshots of Gregor, Demetria and Kristo.

Most were superimposed. But the average person wouldn't know that.

"Gregor will have heard, then," she said. "This is awful!"

He nodded, certain that his elder brother *had* seen and felt the slap of betrayal by now. That both brothers had lost respect for him when news had reached them.

But neither Mikhael nor Gregor had rung him, and he'd been too busy haggling over the best course of action to surmount this scandal to ring them. Once they'd decided what to do, the royal lawyers had thought it prudent that they contact Gregor and advise him how to handle the reporters that were sure to haunt him.

The confrontation with his brothers would come later, and he didn't look forward to their censure at all. Because of his past exploits, it was the council's worry that the people would see this as a battle of siblings over the title and a woman.

A Greek tragedy come to life.

But while the people might view this as a love triangle, he

refused to feed that lie to save face. His pride would not let him pretend something that wasn't, no matter that it would be the easier road to take.

"The council, the royal lawyers and I have agreed that the best way to handle this situation is to issue a public statement. Once you and I publicly deem this matter as petty lies, we will personally tour Angyra and speak with the people directly. That is the swiftest way to regain their support."

"When do we make this announcement?" she asked.

"Tomorrow morning," he said. "I trust you will wear something demure."

Her cheeks turned crimson. "Of course."

This time brittle silence stretched between them. He sighed, aware he was handling this badly.

He should leave. Seek his room. But all he longed for was the comfort of her embrace.

Since he'd left her bed yesterday her exotic scent had tormented him to the point where he'd caught himself thinking of her during the meeting.

She'd been a virgin.

She certainly wasn't the harlot the tabloids painted her to be. But these weren't feudal times. He couldn't wave a sheet from the palace window to prove her innocence.

Yet he wanted to stand up for her, even though he was angry that she'd let him seduce her. His anger failed to hold its sting for long, for the thought of her lying in his arms, of him sinking into her, of knowing no man had ever touched her, kept replaying in his mind.

No woman had ever commanded so much of his thoughts. No woman had ever left him feeling so conflicted. No woman had ever sated his needs like she had.

He held no illusions that would ever change. He was only sure of one thing.

"I want you, Demetria. I need you now."

Her soft lips parted, and undeniable passion blazed in her eyes. "I want you as well."

"Come."

He extended his hand to her, his eyes on hers, his heart beating so frantically he was sure she could hear it. Her throat worked as she laid her hand in his much larger one.

That contact of skin on skin sent an electric current through him that staggered him. He tugged her to him and groaned his pleasure as she molded against him.

"I have waited all day for this moment," he said.

"Me too."

That admission tugged a smile from him.

He led her into her bedroom, noting the covers were smooth. The thought of her dark luscious hair spread over rumpled sheets doubled the heavy ache in his groin.

His mouth swooped down on hers, demanding and possessive, silencing any protest she might make. She hesitated, frozen for a guarded second like a statue captured for all time. Then, with a sweet moan that sang through his veins, she scraped her fingers through his hair and held his head tight, kissing him with the same demanding need.

He'd known Demetria was capable of deep passion, but he'd not expected she'd exhibit such primal lust. This was the earthy sex he'd expect of a mistress, not the woman he was to marry.

With a savage growl, he slid his thumbs under the thin straps of her top and shrugged them off her shoulders. Still it wasn't enough, for he wanted her naked. Wanted her under him now, begging for his possession.

He pulled from her on an oath, and tugged the cotton from her. For the longest moment he just stared at her, awed by the perfectly shaped breasts and rose-tipped nipples that were hard and begging for his touch.

"Beautiful," he murmured, his palms sliding over her firm

pert breasts, and he had the satisfaction of feeling her arch into his hands on a purr that shot a bolt of longing to his sex.

His thumbs scraped over the hardened tips again and again.

The hands clutching his head dropped to his shoulders, the nails digging into his flesh. Her eyes went black.

"It is always this intense for you?" she asked.

He shook his head for, like her, he was tumbling fast into the morass of passion.

"Only with you," he said.

She swayed into him, head lifted and mouth seeking his.

He met her halfway in a kiss that robbed them both of breath, that left no doubt that in this they were well matched, that here there was no arguing, no battle of wills.

He'd never been one to mutter love words with a woman, but with Demetria he felt compelled to openly adore her. It was those little gasps and moans that she made that proved she held back nothing either.

This time he was determined to savor their joining. His hands swept down the graceful arch of her spine to cup the firm globes of her bottom. She strained against him on a moan, and stroked his already engorged shaft against her belly.

"No more waiting," he said.

"No more," she repeated, between kisses that enflamed him more, that matched the need exploding in him.

He couldn't imagine ever tiring of her kisses, her touch.

Her body quaked. And his did as well, for his control was about to explode.

"You're overdressed," she said as she proceeded to undo the buttons on his shirt.

As hot as he was, it was amazing his clothes hadn't burst into flames. He suffered her ministrations for a minute. Then two.

"For a designer, you are ill-suited at removing clothes."

He pulled back enough to grab his shirt and rip it off. Still it seemed to take an eternity for him to shrug off his trousers and shorts.

Chest heaving, he lifted his gaze to hers. Dawn speared through the bank of windows, gilding the room and the shapely curves of her naked body.

No statue in all of Greece could compare to her beauty. None could rival her allure.

She was a goddess to be worshipped. And she was his.

His palms memorized the delicate line of her jaw before he trailed his fingers down her neck, marveling at the silken texture of her skin, the telling rush of color that bloomed in his wake. Though she made no move, the rapid rise and fall of her chest confirmed his effect on her.

"I have dreamed of doing this again," he said, then bent to suckle one pert breast deeply, before doing the same to the other, leaving the buds wet and pebble-hard.

She moaned and arched against him. "I have too."

"And this?" he asked, dropping to his knees as he pressed openmouthed kisses over the flat planes of her midriff and belly, certain he'd never seen skin this firm and yet so soft.

"Yes," she whispered, her nails digging into his back. "Yes."

The womanly scent of her arousal fired his blood, and he fought for control that he'd always taken for granted. His thumbs parted the thatch of dark curls at the apex of her thighs to bare her sweet essence to him. She trembled, gripping his shoulders harder, thrusting her sex closer to him.

He needed no urging. His hands gripped her hips to steady her and he bent to kiss her intimately, deeply.

A sound burst from her, part startled gasp, part sensual moan. It filled him with male satisfaction and left him feeling triumphant.

His tongue showed no mercy, flicking over her womanly folds, thrusting deep into her core that was hot and slick with her own desire. The tight ache in his groin intensified to the point where he broke out in a sheen of sweat.

He'd never felt this way about a woman before. She made him feel young. Desired. Masterful. With her, the feelings swelling within him were all magnified. Larger than life. Much more than he could grasp right now.

Still he pleasured her ruthlessly, stroking the swollen bud until her body trembled. Her legs buckled, her fingers clawing at him now in either desperation or supplication.

But he didn't stop laving the tender flesh, suckling deeply, knowing she was about to shatter in his arms.

That he could give her this much pleasure intensified his own. This went far beyond being a generous lover.

The emotions building inside him were volcanic, unlike any he'd felt before. Being intimate with her felt right.

He didn't want to rush this joining. He wanted to savor every kiss, every caress.

The pain of his need was almost unbearable for him, yet he suffered the wait until she found sweet release. Until she dug her fingers into his shoulders and climaxed.

She came swift and hard, in a tremor that shook her from head to toe. Shaking him in the process.

Her cry echoed in the room in a song that he'd enjoy waking to every morning and falling asleep to every night. At least in this they were compatible. A man in his position couldn't ask for more.

But deep down a voice mocked him, for he'd vowed not to follow in his parents' footsteps.

No choice, he thought. No choice but to forestall a disaster to his country. No other choice that he wanted to consider.

He lifted his head, reality threatening to dim his pleasure.

But that too drifted away on the breeze as she crumbled into his arms, sweet mouth curved in a smile and eyes languorous.

"My God, I never knew it could be like this between a man and a woman." She smiled on a sigh of pleasure that slid over his skin like a heated caress, leaving him trembling with renewed need.

"This is just the beginning, *agapi mou*," he said as he stretched out beside her.

The honeyed taste of her passion lingered on his tongue, an aphrodisiac that sent his senses reeling. Thoughts of duty and revenge foamed like the surf before washing back out to sea.

She was the woman he wanted as his lover. Now and forever.

"You are such a sensuous creature." He grazed a knuckle along her jaw and down the slope of her neck, smiling as her skin pebbled and flushed at this touch.

"You make me sensuous," she said, on a purr that hummed through his veins.

Her words stroked his male ego, but the simple truth that she wasn't experienced thawed the cold that had been buried deep inside him.

He should have realized it that day on the beach. Her hesitation. How she'd followed his lead instead of taking the initiative. How her big innocent eyes had stared up at him in wonder.

Yet he'd turned a blind eye to the obvious. He'd relegated her to the role of a schemer. An unfaithful flirt who'd make his brother's life hell.

He'd been so wrong. He'd wronged her.

"There is so much more to be enjoyed," he said.

A smile of pure pleasure teased her sensual mouth. She pressed a hand over his heart, the small fingers splayed over his skin to set him on fire.

"Show me," she said.

"With pleasure."

Her hands slid over the slope of her pert breasts and he marveled that he couldn't see the sparks that surely crackled in the air from the erotic contact. A nudge of his knees parted her legs without hesitation, yet there was a tenderness to her actions that he'd never experienced before.

It hinted he should take his time to dazzle her with his finesse. He longed to explore every inch of her body, to leave no doubt that she was his. To make love with her all night instead of for a few stolen hours.

His mouth claimed hers in a torrid melding of lips and the parry of tongues. The moist tip of his erection parted her slick swollen folds, the throb reverberating through him in hot urgent pulses that were nearly his undoing.

The needy sounds coming from her left no doubt she was tired of the wait too.

In one powerful surge he sank fully into her, only to pull out just as swiftly. She mewled a protest and arched against him, silken legs wrapped around his waist to pull him back inside her.

He tore his mouth from hers and obliged on a guttural groan. The strain of holding a rein on his raging desire was almost too great for him.

"Please," she whispered, small hands clawing at his arms, his back, before digging into the firm globes of his buttocks.

He needed no other urging.

His hands bracketed her face as he surged into her quivering sheath once more. Her lips parted and her eyelids flickered with the power of her passion.

Again and again their bodies strained in fiery rhythm. He stared into her rapturous eyes, thinking he'd never held anything more precious in his arms.

At that moment he knew she was more priceless to him than all the gold on Angyra. He'd never made love like this before.

And that scared the hell out of him.

Right now he needed to be strong. To think with his head, not his manhood.

With a savage curse, he set a ruthless pace. But even then she moved with him in primal harmony, until he blessedly couldn't think of anything anymore except clutching her close to his heart and finding his own release.

Her back bowed as she reached for nirvana again, his name bursting from her.

He held her tight, his head pounding with the strain of holding back, of letting her savor every second of spent passion.

She collapsed on the bed, the strong muscles of her inner thighs relaxing their hold on his flanks, her hands loosing their tight hold on him.

Only then did he seek his release. His head reared, teeth clenched at the force exploding within him. His blood thundered in his ears, his last coherent thought one of awe at the pleasure flooding him.

He collapsed on her, the valley between her bosom pillowing his head that was too heavy for him to lift. He'd never been this spent.

Or this pleased.

The beginning of a smile twitched at his lips. If only they could hold the world and all the troubles facing them at bay.

CHAPTER EIGHT

DEMETRIA didn't know when Kristo had left her bed, but he returned to her apartment before nine. She had roused earlier, near starving, to find the air filled with the most enticing aromas from the kitchen. A huge dinner must be in order today.

Perhaps this time she would be able to eat.

Or perhaps not.

She didn't look forward to this display today. But she was ready, having chosen a simple silk blouse and a skirt that was classically elegant and not the least bit provocative.

"You look stunning," he said, and bent to kiss her.

"And you are quite handsome." Gorgeous, actually.

He'd have made a sought-after model with his classic good looks and beautifully sculpted body.

Only she noted the deeper lines fanning from his eyes. The tension that kept his shoulders racked tight.

The tolling of bells brought a grim smile from him. "Come. It is time for the announcement."

She was a jumble of nerves by the time they reached the front balcony of the palace—more so because the servants they'd passed had avoided making eye contact with her. It was if they were shunning her. That fear only heaped more guilt on her.

They hate me.

A crowd had gathered below on the street, its silence needling her nerves even more. If Kristo hadn't had such a tight grip on her hand she'd have been tempted to flee back to her room.

He pulled her along with him to the railing. Cameras were raised in the near distance and she forced a smile, knowing she must appear calm when her insides were in knots.

"At present, Demetria Andreou, Prince Gregor and I are the targets of malicious gossip," he said as the paparazzi snapped pictures of them as a couple. "We come to you today to inform you that it is all lies and half-truths. We ask that you remember that my brother is ill, and that by allowing this gossip to flourish we hurt him."

Demi held her breath as murmurs rippled through the crowd, but nobody spouted the questions or curses she'd dreaded to hear. Nobody said anything that could be overheard.

That silence was damning.

Oh, God, the effect her sister's meddling had had on Angyra must be far worse than they'd anticipated.

"And I also ask that you join us as we walk to the cemetery to honor my father on the fortieth day after his death," he said, shocking her with that suggestion.

This time the murmurs became a low rumble. But Kristo didn't tarry on the balcony to hear.

"*Náste Kalá!*" And with that farewell he turned and led her back into the palace.

"Are you crazy?" she asked as she kept pace beside him.

"Probably, but the people need to see us holding to tradition," he said. "We must show honor to my father now, and invite them as witnesses."

She could only imagine the headache this would cause Vasos and his team of bodyguards. "I wish you would have warned me."

He shrugged. "I told you that we'd be out among the people."

"Yes, but I never dreamed you'd suggest we all walk to the cemetery!"

"It's an old tradition, and it will allow the staff to prepare the area before the palace for the feast."

"Feast?" she said, nearly choking on the word.

He flicked her a rare smile, looking very assured. Very much in control. "Once we have paid our respects at the cemetery I've invited the people to join us for a celebration on the front lawn."

Surely it was unheard-of for a King to go to such lengths? Dangerous lengths. But then it was clear that Kristo was a risk-taker.

That would explain all the enticing aromas she'd smelled this morning. "Did the council suggest all this?"

"They stressed that we should become approachable to the people. The idea was mine."

His hand tightened on hers, their fingers entwining. It was a fine show of solidarity. Affection for the people to observe. Except they were still in the palace.

Her gaze flew to his, questioning. The quick squeeze on her fingers was solely for her benefit. A silent encouragement from him to her.

Trust me, the gesture hinted.

She wanted to. Oh, how she wanted to trust him. But it was still too soon.

He paused at the door to accept a huge bouquet of fresh flowers. Then they left the palace by the open-air corridor, but the perfume from the bougainvillea and jasmine that she'd thought pleasant upon arriving seemed cloying to her now.

Vasos and his men formed a cordon to keep the people at bay. Still they seemed so close she could read the doubt in their eyes, the speculation, the anger.

Kristo gave no indication he'd noticed, but she was sure he had. Very little ever got by him.

So they moved like an army toward the church and adjoining cemetery. The King with his head held high and his features carefully masked of emotion. She quite literally quaking, with a horrendous case of nerves and guilt.

Talk was absent, which was a blessing—for she wouldn't have been able to speak coherently. The people pressed around them, but the only sounds were the pounding of feet on the cobblestones and the drumming of her heart.

More people crowded around a cemetery that couldn't possibly hold a fourth of them. So they clustered by the walls and watched.

Kristo stopped beside an ornate tombstone, and Demetria tried her best not to lean into his strength. But when he dropped to a knee before the grave of his father and laid the bouquet on the ground a hush of respect fell over those gathered.

Again he looked invincible. A man in control of himself and his world. But she felt the tremor rocket from him to her. She sensed the grief he silently suffered.

Her eyes filled with tears and she tried desperately to hold them back. But the actions of this proud man touched her as nothing else had. The tears fell in silent rivers and she swiped them away the best she could. She hadn't even thought to grab a tissue.

A scuffle at her right caught her attention. An older woman was doing her best to catch her attention around the burly guard.

"It's for Her Highness," the woman said, loud enough for Demetria to hear this time. In her gnarled hand she held a handkerchief.

"Let her through," Demetria said.

The guard remained unmoved, so Demi pulled her hand

from Kristo's and crossed to the woman. "Thank you," she said to the lady, and took the offered handkerchief to dab the tears from her eyes.

"The gods shined on us the day that the King in his wisdom chose you as future Queen," the old woman said as she executed a bow.

And the reporters who were always present captured the moment on film.

The thought struck Demi that maybe now a new headline would grace the tabloids before nightfall. A picture that commanded respect, with an accompanying story that might make the earlier one stand for what it was—vicious gossip.

Kristo had been right. Her sister had acted cruelly. She hoped that she'd learned her lesson now. That she and Kristo could move forward without more trouble. That in time they would find something more than duty to bind them together.

She felt Kristo beside her long before he took her free hand in his again. She spared him a quick glance, only to find that his devastatingly handsome smile was being given to the older woman.

"*Efharisto,*" he said to the lady, taking her gnarled hand and placing a kiss on the thin wrinkled skin. "You are most kind to come to my future Queen's aid."

"*O Theos mazi sou,*" the older woman wailed, bowing so deeply Demi feared she'd topple over.

That simple blessing from an old woman to the King seemed to break the ice that surrounded the people. Some sobbed. Many coughed to clear their throats.

He turned to Demi and smiled then, and any misgiving she held in her heart instantly thawed. This wasn't an act on his part, to garner sympathy from the people. This was real.

Before her stood a man in control of his emotions. A man

who didn't toss praise or words of endearment out at whim. A man who wasn't afraid to take chances.

Yet winning his love wouldn't be easy. Maybe impossible.

"This has been a troubled few months for the Royal House of Stanrakis," he said, his voice ringing loud and clear. "From the loss of our beloved King, *o sinhoremenos*, to my brother's grave illness. To all of you, *na tous cherese.*"

Echoes of good wishes came from those surrounding them, one by one. She felt some of the tension leave Kristo, felt her heart swell with pride at the manner in which he'd opened himself up to the people.

And that was crucial—for they didn't know him, only his jaded reputation. "That was beautiful," she told him.

He smiled, and she nearly forgot how to breathe. "No, *you* are beautiful."

Before she could savor that compliment, Kristo addressed the crowd. "Please join us at the palace. A feast has been prepared in my father's honor. Enjoy!"

With that, he clasped her hand in his and strode from the cemetery. Back to the palace. Back to the place she would forever call home. And maybe there was a chance they could actually make it one—if Kristo opened up to her, if he gave her a chance to win his heart.

Kristo smiled when they returned to the palace and were greeted by music. Loud. Boisterous. And purely Greek.

Never in his life had he seen the palace lawn turned over to the populace. His father would surely turn over in his grave, but perhaps that was a good thing too.

His family had ruled with a strong hand, but that didn't mean they couldn't have the occasional throwback to earlier times. Especially now, when he needed to feel the pulse of the people. To know if they were on his side or waiting to stab him in the back!

"This is beyond belief," Demetria said as he guided her to a table set apart for them, the council and other dignitaries of Angyra. "Whose idea was this?"

"Mine. I remembered Father saying that death should be celebrated." He glanced at the tables laden with food. Wine and ouzo flowed freely. "I believe he'd approve."

But, whether he would or not, it was obvious that the people were enjoying this side of their royals. It was a bold step to take, and the council and the lawyers had warned him it could backfire, but it worked.

Though he hoped he'd gain the people's favor, or at the very least their interest, it was clear that they were entranced by Demetria. She'd regained their support. Their respect.

And though that came well before his own slow rise in popularity, he found himself smiling as well. She'd charmed them as she did him.

The morning turned to afternoon, and the crowd grew more boisterous. As he and Demetria were dancing the *hassapiko* with five other people, Kristo caught the guarded look on Vasos's face and knew their time at the celebration was over.

To stay would be dangerous—for him and Demetria.

"It is time for us to take our leave," he told her when the dance ended. "Come."

She hesitated for a moment, glancing back at the crowd. He saw the longing in her eyes. Knew that she realized this would be the last time she was able to freely dance and celebrate with the people.

In a few days she'd be royalty.

"I hate to see it end," she said.

"It won't for them." He ran a knuckle along her cheek. "Or for us either, if you don't mind a very private party."

A slow smile played over her kissable mouth, her face flushed from dancing, her eyes sparkling with happiness. "I'd love it."

In moments they'd slipped back inside the palace. They paused in the hall to kiss—a long, hot kiss that fired their blood.

He'd intended to take her to his room, but hers was closer. As it was they barely made to the bedroom before they fell into each other's arms in a frenzy to make love.

Much later, as she lay curled against his side, Kristo tried to wrap his mind around the events of this day. For the first time since he'd gained the crown he felt in control.

With Demetria he simply felt relaxed. Whole. Happy?

A smile teased his mouth. He'd never believed it could be true, but he enjoyed being with her. And not just for sex!

Today among the people it had been nothing short of magical. And tonight...

Tonight he planned to enjoy a quiet dinner with her. After he woke her with a kiss. After he made love with her again.

The trill of his mobile echoed sharply in the velvet twilight. He swore as he rifled through his discarded clothes for it. The number in the display made his blood run cold. His brother.

He answered with a clipped, *"Éla."*

"Gregor is failing quickly," Mikhael said. "There is nothing more that can be done."

It was the worst possible timing, and yet he had no choice but to show a united front—especially in light of the scandal.

"I'll be there as soon as possible."

No more needed to be said.

He ended the call and placed one to his pilot, aware that Demetria had stirred beside him. "Ready the plane. I must leave immediately."

"What's wrong?" she asked, when he dropped the mobile on the table and heaved a frustrated sigh.

"Gregor is dying," he said, the strained emotions making his voice sound rougher than usual. "I must go to him."

"Of course."

She sat up beside him, drawing the sheet around her, looking sad. Nervous.

He rolled from the bed and the temptation her nearness stirred, dressing quickly. It would be so easy to take her in his arms. Hold her. Take the comfort she was clearly ready to give him. But that was how a playboy would behave. Not a King.

"When do we leave?" she asked.

He cut her a frown, surprised she'd assume he was taking her with him. "We? You won't accompany me in this."

"Why? I was betrothed to him since I was twelve."

"You are also the woman who betrayed him with me," he said, annoyed that she seemed eager to flaunt what they'd done before his dying brother.

"He's certain to have heard about this scandal by now. We could tell him the truth together," she said, biting her lower lip, as if uncertain how to go on with this horrible idea. "We could explain how we—"

"No! We will not team up against my brother."

"I wasn't suggesting we do that," she said, her voice holding a quaver of frustration now. "But I'm the woman Gregor was betrothed to for ten years."

"Which is why you will not be there," he said. "You betrayed him, Demetria. There is no explanation for that."

She reeled back against the headboard of the bed, eyes wide and stark, face far too pale. "I disagree. I want to see him."

In three steps he was at the bedside and had pulled her up against him. Mistake!

He realized it as the sheet fell from her, as her lush breasts molded against his chest and the flames of desire licked over them. That was not what he wished to be tormented with when he faced his dying brother!

He narrowed his gaze on her too luminous eyes, angry she had this power over him. "Why? What possible explanation can you give a dying man? That you fell into lust with me?"

"If you're honest with yourself, you'll admit there was a magnetic pull that we couldn't resist."

"We will not flaunt our lust in front of my brothers. Don't press me on this again."

"Dammit, Kristo! It was more than that!"

"What? Surely you won't claim that you fell in love?"

"Of course not! That would be the last thing I would feel for you," she said, shoving her fists between them and breaking his hold.

He glared at her, chest heaving with annoyance while his heart ached with worry. Again he was handling this wrong with her, but he didn't have time to explain his feelings to her now.

"I'll keep you informed," he said.

She gave a jerky nod, but didn't look at him.

That was the image of her that stayed with him as he raced to the airport.

Thirty minutes later Kristo stood at his brother's bedside and executed a deep bow of respect. "I came as quickly as I could."

Yet the flight from Angyra to Athens had never seemed to long or so fraught with anxiety. He'd had no idea what he'd walk into, yet he was determined to meet his fate without complaint.

Gregor's lips pulled in a weak smile and his glazed eyes lifted to his. "Thank you, my King. Though I told Mikhael not to trouble you."

"I wouldn't have forgiven him if he hadn't called me," Kristo said, flicking his younger brother the barest smile of gratitude.

But the greeting wasn't returned. Mikhael simply stared at him with cool dark eyes. *He knew.* Kristo was certain Mikhael was aware of the brewing scandal. Gregor as well?

The answer came a heartbeat later. "I see we have made headlines in all the gossip rags," Gregor said. "Is there any truth to it?"

He could lie. Save his brother hurt. But he'd hate anyone to do that to him.

And so he told his brother with an economy of words exactly what had happened that day on the beach, leaving out details of their intimacy.

"It is hard to tell who was more shocked that night at the palace when we realized each other's identity," Kristo said. "I never intended to betray you, nor did she. It just happened."

His brothers fell silent. A brooding silence for Mikhael. With Gregor he couldn't tell. Like their father, he was adept at cloaking his emotions.

"Did you sleep with her?" Gregor asked at last.

"Not while she was betrothed to you."

Gregor gave a clipped nod. "It is good, then, that you are the one who will marry her."

"Enough about my indiscretion. What of your condition?" he asked Gregor. "I can't accept that nothing more can be done to help you. That we gather around your bed and wait."

"I've brought in the leading authorities on his condition," Mikhael said, his expression grim. "It is out of our hands."

He'd known it the moment he'd walked into the room, yet conceding defeat left a sour taste on his tongue. He had lost his father forty days ago. He didn't want to lose his brother too.

The brother he'd betrayed. That would always be his cross to bear.

The anger he heaped on Demetria for betraying Gregor was twofold on himself. In his heart, he knew he didn't deserve the crown.

Gregor gasped, teeth clearly clenched in pain for an agonizing moment. When it ended his complexion had turned a cooler gray.

"Forgive me. I didn't want to die before the wedding," Gregor said, gasping for breath again. "I wanted to see my playboy brother claim his royal bride. To see Angyra celebrate its King and Queen."

"I will endeavor to do my best for our country," Kristo said. "But in light of your failing health I should postpone the wedding."

"No," Gregor said, his tone authoritative and yet so weak. "Do not mourn me. Angyra has suffered enough through Father's death. They do not need another one so soon afterward."

"You know that you are still much favored in Angyra."

"That doesn't matter," he said, his voice barely a whisper now. "You are the King. I believe you will be a far better one than I, for you know how to make Angyra stronger."

He hoped his brother was right. Hoped he'd make a strong leader and a fair one.

"Rest, Gregor," he ordered.

"I will soon. The doctors tell me that I have only hours, not days left to live."

Kristo had known that before he came here, yet hearing it, seeing the proof of his brother's decline, tore at his heart. His family could buy anything they wished. Demand that a kingdom bow to their will. Yet they were helpless against this.

"Go home, my King," Gregor said. "Marry as planned. *Nása kalá!*"

Those words hung in the brittle air as Gregor succumbed

to the inevitable. A nurse rushed forward to check his vitals, then quietly unplugged the monitors and left the room.

Left him and Mikhael flanking the bed where their dead brother lay. Kristo coughed to clear the emotion clogging his throat, knowing he'd lost the chance to gain forgiveness or damnation from Gregor.

Mikhael heaved a sigh. "So what do we do with our brother now?"

"The only thing we can do without regret. Return to Angyra with him and hold a state funeral."

CHAPTER NINE

THE loud steady thud of hammering brought Demetria out of a sound sleep. She sat up and gathered the bedclothes to her bare bosom, realizing that the sound was coming from outside.

Yesterday seemed like a lifetime away now. Had they really danced on the lawn with the people of Angyra, acting like children? Acting free? Had they made love the whole afternoon?

Had she irrevocably lost her heart to Kristo?

It was all true. The memories flooding back to her were very real, as was the tenderness in her breasts and between her legs.

Yet tempering her pleasure was the extreme sadness that came from Gregor's death. Kristo had rung her late last night, saying only that his brother's struggle was over and that they'd return home today.

She dragged herself into the shower. Moments later, as she donned capris and a T-shirt, she heard voices in the salon. She padded to the connecting door and yanked it open, thinking Kristo had returned.

Instead she found Vasos and the maid, surrounded by garment bags and boxes.

Demetria poked her head out her bedroom door, her curiosity too great to remain hidden. "What's going on?"

The maid whirled toward her, a smile wreathing her round face. "The remainder of the wedding finery has arrived."

Demi's questioning gaze lifted to Vasos. Though she'd designed the royal wedding gown, there were a few accessories that needed to be provided. But this array of boxes and garment bags went far beyond the need for satin pumps and undergarments.

"The King has asked that you select your trousseau," he said.

She caught the names emblazoned on the boxes and bags and knew there was a small fortune in clothing here. All top designers that she'd studied with envy.

The *crème de la crème* of those she admired professionally and had hoped to emulate one day. Kristo couldn't have known that, though, for she'd never been able to afford anything made by them.

She forced a smile, even though this order felt like salt being rubbed into a wound. He hadn't done this because he cared for her and wanted to gift her with the best. No, this was part of her new role. The future Queen *must* present herself in only the best.

Still, he could have asked her opinion.

"Fine. Leave them and I'll look through them later," she said, her toner sharper then she'd intended.

Vasos inclined his head. "As you wish. Is there anything you require?"

She shook her head. "What's all the commotion outside?"

"Preparations are under way for the royal wedding."

The moment Vasos took his leave, she crossed to the French doors and watched the small army of workers below. Gardeners were planting a row of roses along the perimeter wall, and the breeze from the sea brought their spicy scent to her.

Other workers were setting up an altar at the edge of the garden wall, their hammering remaining steady. It was a perfect location for a wedding.

Beyond the wall the ground dropped off sharply, to leave a stunning view of the azure sea and the city below. This wedding would be photographed and talked about for eons.

She couldn't think of a more lovely place to hold the ceremony. She'd always wanted to have a garden wedding. Always known that the ivory gown of her heart would glow warmly under a full sun.

And now it would. The fairy-tale wedding, right down to a handsome King at her side.

Her heart ached. Except he didn't love her.

She glanced at the designer garments the maid was carefully removing from the boxes. They could wait. She had one small detail to complete on her wedding gown first.

Kristo stepped inside Demetria's suite to find the maid returning a stack of garments to boxes. He guessed these were the ones Demetria didn't want—which seemed to be most of them.

"Your Majesty," the maid said, and bowed, flicking nervous glances to the bedroom and then back at him.

He gave her an impatient smile and canted his head to the door. "I need a moment of privacy with the lady."

Without a word, the maid scurried from the room.

"What was that?" Demetria said as she strode from the bedroom.

She froze in a pool of sunlight that transformed the gown into a glistening ivory cloud. She looked more luminous than a pearl, a vision that no man would ever forget.

He certainly wouldn't.

"Oh!"

She grabbed a multicolored shawl off the divan and held

it in front of her. But the image of her in her wedding gown was already branded on his mind.

He'd never seen a more beautiful woman in his life, even with the bright drape concealing her. Her tanned skin glowed warmly and her eyes were huge and filled with the same desire that pounded in his veins.

In this they were well matched. He'd never tire of her. Never cease to be awed by her beauty.

Without a doubt nobody would be able to tear their gazes from her at the wedding. She'd simply be the most raved about bride in all of the Mediterranean.

And she'd be his.

He never took his eyes off her radiant face, wondering again why his brother had never been enamored of her. Had it been because of his ill health? Or was it chemistry?

"It's bad luck for you to see the bride in her gown," she said as she backed toward the bedroom.

"Perhaps we've already reached our quota of ill fate."

A flush skimmed across her high cheekbones and strands of her glorious hair escaped the band at her nape to dance around her bare shoulders. The vivid memory of that hair teasing his bare heated flesh tormented him, and he wanted nothing more than to strip them both naked again and lose himself in her willowy arms.

"I don't care to take that chance," she said. "Did you just return?"

"About thirty minutes ago. I've not told the people about Gregor yet." He snorted. "Gregor didn't want me to tell them at all!"

"They should know."

His gaze fixed on hers, and he caught the sheen of moisture and knew its cause. Sorrow. "You realize this means a change in the wedding plans?"

"I suspected as much," she said, her voice solemn. Resigned. "We've no choice."

Choice. He'd given her damned little. And seeing her now in her finery, knowing she'd created something so magnificent, boggled his mind.

"I've arranged to make the announcement of Gregor's death at six," he said. "I'll come for you thirty minutes before."

"I'll be ready."

Again that unnerving spate of silence.

"Would you send the maid in?" she said at last.

"She's gone," he said. "I sent her away."

"What? I need her to help me get out of the gown."

He smiled, thinking that was a task he'd take great pleasure in doing. "I can do that."

"The buttons are tiny."

He lifted one dark eyebrow. "Do you doubt my agility?"

"No, but that means you'll have to see me in the gown again." Her frustrated sigh echoed around him. "Please, will you call the maid in?"

He shook his head and crossed to her bedroom, surprised that she clung to such superstition. He stopped at the door. "No. I'll close my eyes. All you have to do is present your back to me."

"You promise not to look?" she asked.

"Yes." He closed his eyes, agreeing to open them only when she was out of that gown and feeling like a child playing a game.

"All right."

He felt the swish of her skirt against his legs and sucked in a breath at the heightened charge of desire not seeing her created. All his senses were suddenly more attuned, and thoughts of a child's game vanished in a heartbeat.

Her jasmine scent was more provocative. The silken wisps of her hair were softer than the expensive cloth.

Just brushing his fingertips against the smooth curve of her spine as he worked the tiny buttons free awakened his desire. In his mind's eye he saw that wedge of creamy skin that was slowly revealed with each slip of a button.

"Lovely," he said, when he'd slipped the last button free.

"Thank you."

Before she could move away, he skimmed both palms up her spine, parting the gown in his wake. She gasped and he opened his eyes then, looking not at the silk that barely clung to her but at the tanned flesh arrowing to her waist.

Desire roared through his veins, hot and needy. Without a word he pushed the garment off her.

She caught it and stepped free of the skirt, facing him with the silk clutched in her hands, giving him more than a teasing peek of her full bare breasts. "I'll be a moment getting dressed."

"Don't." He followed her into the bedroom.

He lowered his face to hers and grazed her lips once, twice. The third time she strained upward to meet him, losing her grip on the gown to slip her arms around his neck.

Their lips melded in a frisson of fiery need that roared through his blood in a flood of need. His tongue stroked hers with bold intent. He was desperate to keep a hold on his control but it was a losing effort, for he was weary of this constant standoff. Of being her adversary when all he wanted to be was her lover. Her only lover.

She gripped his shirtfront and treated him to the same erotic kisses, the sweet sensuous assault dragging a groan from the depths of his soul.

"You are a vixen," he said against her lips.

She splayed her fingers on his face in a possessive caress. "Only with you, Kristo."

It didn't matter if that was the truth, or if she was just telling him that to appease him. She was his now. The perfect match for him in bed, for she challenged him there as well. And he was ready to prove that point right now.

She smiled against his lips. "How interesting that you had no trouble getting me out of the gown."

"That's because I prefer you naked."

His hands cupped her shoulders to push her from him, just enough so he could appreciate her beauty. The blush tips of her bared breasts thrust upward, begging him to sample. A very sexy red satin thong just barely hid the secrets he longed to explore again at leisure.

"That is a pleasant surprise any groom would appreciate," he said.

She blushed, and again he was struck with the anomaly of her coyness. "It wasn't intentional."

He couldn't care less if she'd planned it or not. Another need roared through him now, demanding satisfaction. Demanding release.

He tore off his shirt and swept her into his arms. Long determined strides carried her to the bed.

She gave him a teasing smile.

He made quick work of stripping off his clothes, trying to find the words that she'd long to hear. All the while her wide luminous eyes caressed him, causing his blood to boil and his lungs to burn with want of her.

Seeing her lying there with her ripe body begging for his mouth and questing hands fogged his reasoning. When his gaze lowered to that tiny scrap of red satin between her legs logic evaporated like sea mist.

His fingers grasped her slender ankles and spread her legs wide. "I have dreamed of this all day," he said as he stretched out between her creamy thighs.

He skimmed his hands up her long legs to the red thong, gliding his thumbs under the edge to stroke her moist swollen flesh. An arrogantly pleased smile touched his mouth. She was ready for him. She was always ready for him.

"So sexy," he said as he pressed a kiss on the transparent satin.

Her fingers dove through his hair and held fast. "Please..."

"Whatever the lady wants," he said.

He tugged the scrap of satin aside and kissed her, lightly at first. Then his tongue plundered. Using the lacy thong as a sensual torment. Taking all she had to give. Forcing her to give more. Testing his own limits as he'd never done before.

She bucked and let out a needy moan, rocking against him in a fast rhythm that made the pain of waiting almost unbearable. Such sweet torture!

Sweat beaded his brow from his effort to hold his desire in check. Still he kept up his ruthless seduction, for he'd never received such joy from watching a woman climax.

Never felt this warmth that expanded in his heart.

She arched her back and cried out her release and he smiled, pleased that he'd given her such pleasure.

Heart pounding a savage beat, he slid his thumbs under the satin triangle to hook the lace band. He dragged it down her legs and tossed it aside, his breathing labored as if he'd run uphill.

"Beautiful," he said as he stroked the creamy skin of her inner thighs.

She reached for him, her fingers closing around his length in sweet torment. "So are you."

He smiled at that, for while lovers had touted his prowess none had ever dared to call a prince beautiful. But Demetria dared that and more.

Her boldness in that regard drew him as surely as the passionate promise glowing in her eyes.

He sprawled atop her quivering body. Their lips met in a crush of raw desire.

"My God," she whispered against his mouth as she scraped her fingernails along his jaw.

The sensual jolt shot through him like a lightning strike. "How do you do it?" he asked, his voice raw as his emotions.

Passion-dazed eyes lifted to his. "Do what?"

"Drive me wild with wanting you."

He didn't wait for her answer. He couldn't wait another second to make her his, to bind them together once more.

She clawed at his back, as if trying to crawl under his skin. And wasn't she there already?

The thought came and went as need consumed him like a firestorm. They moved as one, this time as special as the first time, as exciting as the one that would follow.

But he made love with her as if it would be the last time. And deep in his heart he acknowledged that it very well might be.

Demetria clung to his sweat-slicked body, knowing he'd dozed off, knowing she only had to shove him to get him off her. But the weight of his powerful body was a welcome blanket after the intensity of their mating.

Her thoughts tumbled into a conflicting whirl of sensations. The incredible freedom she'd felt dancing with the people. Making love to Kristo deep into the night. And the simple pleasures like holding his hand.

She could easily delude herself into thinking he loved her. But he didn't.

He'd been honest about that from the start. He wasn't "victim" to that particular emotion.

She still didn't know why he shied away from love. Why he couldn't give her more than sex.

"Who soured you on love?" she asked, but her only answer was his breathing that had finally evened out in sleep.

But she was wide awake, her mind troubled. She'd tried hard to deny what she was feeling. But she couldn't any longer.

The depth of emotions rocketing through her were far beyond anything she'd experienced. More powerful than anything she'd ever dreamed of having.

This was more than sex. Much, much more. And that made it more horrible to bear, for what she felt would not be returned.

Love. She hadn't wanted this consuming need that left her fearing she'd die if she lost him. As if she only felt whole when she was with him. This feeling reduced her to a needy woman who tried to convince herself that she could be content with just his physical love.

It was a lie. She needed more than that from him. She needed his heart. His trust.

But she knew she'd get neither. Knew she was in for heartache because she loved him. Deeply. More deeply than any woman should love a man.

"Damn you, I didn't want this to happen," she whispered, tears stinging her eyes as she glided her hands down the muscles in his back that had finally lost their steel. "But it did."

CHAPTER TEN

KRISTO pushed inside Demetria's suite promptly at a quarter till six, wondering if she'd be ready, as he'd asked. If all went as planned the church bells would begin ringing fifteen minutes from now. The last time they'd tolled was when Gregor had had to gather the people to announce that the King had died.

To his surprise, she stood by the open balcony door wearing a royal blue dress that hugged her curves and ended in a swirl just above her knees. It was fashionable, yet sophisticated.

Her glorious hair hung in loose curls, and he couldn't think of a more fitting crown for such beauty. If only she wasn't frowning.

He strode to her and wished that circumstances had been different. Being at crossed swords with his bride was not the way to start a marriage.

His hand grasped hers and she trembled as if shocked. He felt the electrical charge arc into him like a lightning bolt and set fire to the desire that never truly banked.

Touching her was dangerous, for it narrowed his thoughts to one thing—pleasuring her. But he couldn't stop himself. He, who always remained cool, had discovered his weakness. Her!

He lifted her hand and dropped a kiss on the silken skin.

She couldn't contain her whispered moan. He just managed to still his answering groan.

Amazing how a private moment with her could fast escalate out of control. How all he could think of was taking her back to bed.

He stared at the delicate hand resting in his and marveled at the nimble fingers that created such beauty with beads and lace and silk. Slender fingers that had played over his flesh in long lusty strokes to the point where he'd been nearly mad with wanting her.

With a muttered oath directed at himself, he shook off the carnal images that had his blood roaring in his veins and focused on the task at hand. Within the hour, the Royal House of Stanrakis would officially be in mourning again.

Their marriage would be postponed. His personal life put on hold. But before that happened there was one thing he'd neglected to do for her. And that was causing him more anxiety than he'd believed possible.

"You're scaring me, Kristo," she said, her hands tightening on his when he stood before her, staring.

He was scaring himself, for he'd never traveled this road before. God willing, he would never have to do so again.

He managed a smile and looked into eyes that were wide with concern. "I am honored and pleased that you will be my bride. My Queen," he said, and slid a ring on her finger.

The fit was perfect. She was perfect.

"It's beautiful," she said.

It was priceless, but it paled in comparison to her beauty. "It was commissioned for your wedding."

Her gaze jerked to his. "This is the ring Gregor was to give me?"

"Technically, yes, though he never ordered it made or saw it once it was completed."

"I don't understand."

"Gregor asked me to handle this very personal task for him, claiming he had no talent for such things." So, without knowing the likes and dislikes of their future Queen, just remembering the passion she'd exuded, he'd had the ring designed for her.

That had been a horrendous task, for at the time he'd thought the very worst of her. Still, guilt made a man do the impossible at times.

He'd chosen a three-carat blue diamond surrounded by smaller brilliants because it was spectacular. He'd commissioned the ring to be set in Rhoda gold and platinum as well, to symbolize two of the richest ores on earth. The combination was striking. Just as she was too beautiful for words.

But he'd not known until now that the fire in the blue diamond would match the glow of passion in her eyes before she climaxed. Or that the bands of gold and platinum would bring out the warmth in her light olive skin.

"Do you like it?" he asked, for if she hated it he'd have another one created.

Her lips trembled. Firmed. "It's more than lovely."

She blinked away the sudden moisture that seemed intent on filling her eyes, but it was a useless battle.

"Why tears over something so small?" he asked, uneasy around her when she was like this.

She sniffled, and dabbed at her eyes with the tissue he handed her, looking small and miserable. "Don't you see? It's not the ring. It's all of it together that makes this so heartbreaking."

"All of what? You're making no sense."

"Of course you wouldn't understand. You have seen that I have the gown of my dreams. A garden wedding that is picture-book perfect. I have a devastatingly handsome King as my groom, and now this—a magnificent engagement ring." Though her crying had stopped, two tears slipped from her big sad eyes. "And it's all show. I've gone from being the chosen fiancé of your brother to yours. There's no love."

He heaved a sigh. Love again.

"That's it, then? You would be happy if I professed my undying affection?"

She shook her head. "I wouldn't believe you, for you would only be telling me what I want to hear."

He couldn't deny it, though he was tempted to.

"I wanted you since the first day I met you on the beach," he said, and managed a tight smile when she blinked in surprise.

"Wanted me? As in desired me as a sexual partner? Lusted after me? Is that it?"

"Yes, and if you are honest with yourself you will admit that you are just as desirous of me."

She jerked her gaze from his—as if the truth stung, as if the sight of him sickened her. "How can you be so cold?"

"It is honesty, Demetria. In my position I can't afford to be a victim of emotions."

He didn't understand the sense of loss that settled over him. He sure as hell didn't *want* this weakness, so he shoved those troubling emotions to the back of his mind.

He was the King. He had to make tough decisions for the good of Angyra. He couldn't let one small woman disrupt his life and his kingdom.

Their plans had been made and they would abide by them. *Even if he hated what he was about to do.*

His fingers closed around hers and he ground his teeth when she stiffened. "Come. It's time to make the announcement."

She nodded and fell into step beside him, looking regal and composed, yet far too aloof. Still, that electric thrill shot through him just at having her beside him.

But this time he sensed a wall going up between them. A barrier that might not be as easy to breach.

The moment they reached the main hallway leading to the balcony she abruptly stopped, forcing him to do the same. Much of the staff stood along the walls in a show of support.

"Your Majesty," Vasos said, and bent in a courtly bow.

Both lines of servants followed suit.

He nodded, momentarily regretting that when he'd taken the crown the familiarity he'd shared with these people all his life had changed. This was not the life he wanted, yet he was surprised that accepting the burden no longer angered him.

He guided her toward the door that glowed in the late-afternoon sun.

"Your father will arrive late tomorrow for the funeral," he said, and swore under his breath when she stiffened.

"I don't look forward to that visit," she said in an undertone.

"Nor do I, but protocol demands it."

They'd reached the front balcony, and the cluster of guards and staff made further talk impossible. The doors were opened wide and a roar went up from the crowd that extended from the cobbled lane in front of the palace down to the harbor.

The bells were nearly deafening here, but he knew they'd stop soon. Knew that once he stepped out on that balcony and made the announcement his life would take another huge change.

Finally the tolling stopped, but its echo vibrated off the verdant hills for long minutes. Before the last reverberation died, he grasped Demetria's hand in his and walked out on the balcony.

A large crowd had gathered to throw up a shout of welcome. The enormity of the moment wasn't lost on Kristo.

He'd stood back all his life while his father had come out here to speak to the people first. Always after state and family deaths. Always for national celebrations.

Gregor had stood by their father's side, and Kristo had been content to be in their shadow. He'd had the life he ached to pursue, and being the second son had afforded him that luxury.

Now he was King. Duty came first.

"Marry for love," his mother had told him.

Yet here he stood with his chosen bride, poised to start their marriage with animosity instead of affection.

He glanced at her, and his heart lurched with an empathy that had never been strong in his gene pool. She stared unseeing at the sea of cheering people, their din so loud he could barely hear himself think.

This was just another burden his title carried. He hoped she realized now that they'd always be on display with the people. That the celebration the other day had been a fluke.

He bent close to her ear. "Smile, Demetria. You look like I have a gun in your back."

"In a way you do," she quipped, but the inviting bow of her lips curved into a smile, albeit a tense one.

He swore under his breath and knew there was no help for it. Even if he could find the words there was no time for them right now.

With a hand raised for silence, he stepped to the railing with Demetria by his side. "The Royal House of Stanrakis is grateful for your patience and respect these past few troubled weeks. I deeply appreciate that you joined us in celebrating my father's death."

And now Gregor was gone. His chest tightened at the thought of his brother slipping into obscurity, as he'd wished.

He stared at the gathering. Their silence was palpable. Then, like the tide rolling to the shore, the low rumble of rapid conversation came from those gathered. A few clapped their hands, the applause slow but building.

"Hail to the future King and Queen of Angyra," a man in the crowd shouted, and soon others joined in with well wishes.

If there were any detractors—and he was sure there were those who found this turn of events unsatisfactory—they wisely kept their opinions to themselves.

"Wave and smile as if you are thrilled beyond words, for it's clear they hold you in high regard," said Kristo.

He felt a tremor go through Demetria as she lifted a hand and waved. Not the cursory movement he'd seen some royals make. But a genuine greeting. One that she'd give to a friend across the street.

"I'm the same person I was yesterday, when I was dancing with them," she said.

But that wasn't true. Up here she was the future Queen.

"As you all are aware, the royal wedding was to take place in the formal garden next Saturday," he said, pausing to let a ripple of agreement go through those gathered. "Unfortunately tragedy has struck the Royal House of Stanrakis again and the wedding must be postponed. Prince Gregor, my beloved brother, is dead."

Behind him, Mikhael's low voice reached him as he comforted an elderly aunt. Women wept. Men moaned.

Demetria stood quietly at his side. His comfort.

Kristo stood tall and firm, his heart clenched with grief. He had done what duty decreed, even though it went against Gregor's wishes.

This was the right thing to do for Angyra. For him and Demetria as well? Only time would tell.

He wanted the people to accept her. To forget that she'd been Gregor's betrothed. To love her as much as he did.

That admission gave him pause. Was that why he thought

of her every second? Why he had to touch her if he was near her? Why she haunted his sleep with her beguiling smile?

Had he fallen in love with her?

CHAPTER ELEVEN

THE dinner was more elegant than she could have imagined, and far more somber than any meal should be. Demetria sat at the opposite end of a lacquered dining table from Kristo, wishing she knew the workings of his mind. But he'd said nothing to her, leaving her to feel like one of the pieces of art on display.

She wished she knew what was troubling him. Wished she could have had a moment alone to speak with Kristo. But since the announcement his family, friends and royal dignitaries had demanded his attention. She had been pushed aside, forgotten or ignored—she wasn't sure which.

Even now, at the long dining table, a dozen of his cousins and close family members carried on hushed conversations that she failed to grasp. His brother Mikhael sat at her left, far more reserved than she remembered him being.

An elegant young woman who was the daughter of a council member had taken the chair on Kristo's left and captured his attention with soulful looks, softly spoken words that forced him to bend close to her, and repeatedly touched his hand in a gesture of sympathy that lingered far too long.

The last troubled her, for it was blatantly clear that the woman had eyes only for Kristo. Thankfully none of the other guests had seemed to notice but her.

"I was convinced that you were a gold digger, but I have

been proved wrong," Mikhael said, his voice a rich purr that was pleasing but lacked the sensual quality of Kristo's. "I was also certain you hated my brother, but I can see that isn't the case."

Demetria glared at him, which gained her his rogue's smile, and chose to ignore the first remark. "I do hate him at times."

Mikhael arched a dark brow, clearly not believing her.

He leaned so close she could smell the brandy on his breath. "I know a jealous woman when I see one, and you, Demetria, are jealous."

"Rubbish," she said, and took a sip of her wine in what she hoped was a nonchalant manner.

He gave a careless shrug. "Deny it all you wish, but it is the truth."

He was right. She loved Kristo. She was jealous. Furiously jealous of him, and simply furious with the woman seated beside him for her blatant flirtation.

"Of course he is the same," Mikhael said.

She glanced at him over her wineglass. "He's possessive. That is not the same thing."

"I shall prove you wrong." Mikhael pushed to his feet and instantly garnered everyone's attention. "It is too beautiful an evening to spend inside cloaked in grief. So I have invited my future sister-in-law to join me for a walk in the garden."

He extended a hand to her, his smile utter charm. The guests were so quiet she was sure they could hear her heart race like the wind.

She was caught between insulting him by refusing his offer in front of his family, or leaving the woman and Kristo alone. Neither option appealed to her.

Truthfully, she wanted to get away, because the past two hours had been a dreadful strain to endure. She had never been so besieged by such a torrent of opposing emotions.

"What a splendid idea," the woman at Kristo's right said, breaking the silence.

Demi's gaze fixed on the woman's smug smile. Like a volcano, anger boiled inside her again and threatened to spew.

Getting out of here was her only option. If she stayed, she'd surely make a scene.

She laid her linen aside and rose, hoping a walk in the fresh air would clear her head and cool her temper. "I agree."

"As do I," Kristo said, on his feet and striding toward Demi before she could place her hand on Mikhael's arm. "Come, *agapi mou.*"

Upon hearing him voice that endearment in public one of his elderly aunts bobbed her head and let out a pleased sigh.

If only the words held meaning for him. The fierce gleam in his dark eyes was deep and troubled. Yes, he was possessive, but there was some other emotion there that she'd not seen before—something primal and fathomless.

"Shall we?" Kristo asked.

She inclined her head, for truly she didn't trust herself to speak right now. Kristo pressed his hand to the small of her back and she burned with need.

Being alone with him would lead to the bedroom. It always did. For the life of her she couldn't think of a reason to refuse him. It was a shameful admission to make in the wake of Gregor's death, but she couldn't deny it.

"Thank you all for coming, and for your support," he told the guests. "Now, if you'll excuse us?"

All of the guests smiled and demurred to their King and future Queen. All but the woman next to Kristo, whose eyes snapped with anger.

Demetria looked away, relieved when Kristo escorted her from the palace. The balmy night air carried the salty tang of the sea and the spicy scent of jasmine and bougainvillea.

But tension held her in its grip as the day's events played over and over in her mind, leaving her chilled in spirit.

Lights from the various shops along the cliff cast swaths of color over the dark water, making it appear as if a rainbow of ribbons had been unfurled. But the spectacular vista afforded her failed to capture her interest as Kristo slid his arms around her and pulled her close.

Her world narrowed to him and her. She splayed her palms over his warm broad chest and the taut planes of muscle that she'd explored at leisure last night. It would be so easy to cuddle against him.

"I never realized you had such a large family," she said. "That will take getting used to."

"Those are the close ones. There are three times that many with distant cousins." He nudged her chin up with his fingers, his eyes near black in the diffused light. Deep. Mysterious. "What of your family? All you've mentioned is your father and sister."

For good reason! She was loath to admit she came from a dysfunctional family. "That's about it. My father was an only child, and his parents are both dead," she said. "My stepmother was adopted, and after she passed we never heard from her family again."

"What of your mother's people?"

"They disowned her, and subsequently me."

"Because of the scandal?"

She nodded, feeling oddly relieved that she'd finally told someone about her past. It was a very bitter pill to swallow, knowing that your family wanted no part of you, even though you'd done nothing wrong.

"They are fools," he said, and she smiled at the heat in his tone.

"My grandfather was of noble Greek blood, and his daughter's actions were unforgivable. To know she'd given herself to an Italian, especially a married man, when she was betrothed to another noble Greek brought great shame on their family."

"Yet they married her off to your father," he said, proving he remembered the scandal.

"Father said that only my mother's father attended the wedding," she said. "After that day they never heard from her family again."

"Even when your mother died?"

She shook her head. "Not a word. For to them she'd been dead for a year. As for me—Father suspected they believed I was the bastard child of her lover."

But she wasn't, and it shamed her to admit that there had been times when she'd wished it were so—that she was anyone's daughter other than Sandros Andreou's.

"It is unfathomable that they've never been a presence in your life," he said.

"Well, I was told that my grandfather left a trust fund for me. But I can't touch it until I marry and produce an heir." She grimaced. "A Greek heir."

"Yes, very traditional."

She didn't bother to add that she didn't want her grandfather's money. He hadn't wanted her when she was a child in need of love. He was not welcome in her life now.

Kristo's beautiful mouth pulled into a tight, disagreeable line again. "Did you know that a wedding invitation has been sent to them?"

"No. But then I was never consulted about the guest list," she said, wanting to be angry at him over this slight, but simply not finding the energy to fight it any longer. "I know. Protocol demands that you invite them."

He made a gruff sound and nudged her chin up, eyes glittering with an emotion she'd not seen before. "Very true. But remember one thing, *agapi mou*. After we are married, they will bow to you."

"I don't care if they do," she said.

"I do," he said, pressing a fierce kiss on her mouth that stunned as well as warmed her. "You'll be my Queen, and as such you'll command respect."

She managed a small smile, knowing he'd never understand that respect was the last thing she wanted.

Love.

That was what she wanted most from him.

"Do you know you've never told me about *your* childhood or your mother?" she said, hoping he would now.

He heaved a sigh and pulled her down beside him on a bench. "It wasn't a typical childhood, but it was all we knew. Mother was busy with her duties, and so was Father, so we were basically raised by nannies."

"I can imagine you giving them a merry chase in this huge palace," she said.

He laughed, the sound so rare she just stared at him. "We were boisterous when we were young, with all the energy boys can hold, but after Gregor turned eight he was pretty much segregated from us."

"Why?"

"He was the Crown Prince," he said, as if that explained it all. "Father made sure that his duties were pounded into him. So for the most part it was just Mikhael and me."

How sad that Gregor had lost that closeness with his siblings, that he'd been denied a childhood because of the order of his birth. "So what was it like growing up here for you and your younger brother?"

"I wanted for nothing, and neither did Mikhael. We had a huge playroom to ourselves, and a nanny who fussed after us. When I turned eight I was sent away to boarding school in Greece," he said.

And she thought she'd had a wretched childhood! "That's too young to be sent away! And, while I can understand the need for a nanny, what of your parents? What role did they play in your life?"

He shrugged, an abrupt movement that screamed of pent-up tension. This was not a subject he cared to discuss!

"My parents were the King and Queen," he said. "We didn't have a close relationship with our parents. They were simply too busy for that."

"People who are too busy with their own lives shouldn't have children."

He was silent for a long moment. "You'd give up your career or duty for your family?"

"Yes! Children need to know that their parents love them, support them, in order to thrive," she said.

"How can you say that after you've admitted that you were little more than your stepmother's helper? That your father was so greedy that he used you, his daughter, to further himself?"

She reeled back, stung by the venom in his tone. It would be easy to cave in. To leave him to his delusions. But pride refused to turn a blind eye to his assumptions.

"My father is many things—brutal, greedy and at times obnoxiously loud—but I never doubted he loved me, that he believed he was doing the best for me by securing my marriage to the Crown Prince," she said.

He snorted, as if discounting her words as nothing. "And your sister's mother? Would you have me believe that she treated you the same as her own flesh and blood?"

"Believe what you will," she said. "The truth is that she was the one who taught me to sew, who nurtured my feeble attempts to create something by myself. Because of her encouragement when I was young, and her praise when I succeeded, I rushed through my studies at university to begin my career, well aware that time was short before I'd be forced to honor my duty to your crown."

His fingers entwined with hers, and for the first time she didn't feel any jolt of passion. Instead of that sizzle of desire she'd come to dread and crave in turn, she felt incredibly sad that he'd never experienced the love she had.

"You put too much stock in love," he said.

"And you put none in it."

He didn't deny it, and that made her heart ache all the more for him. For a brief moment she glimpsed the little boy who'd craved affection. Then in a blink he reverted to the arrogant man who denied the need for love.

"It's been a very long day," he said, and rose, dragging her up as well. "It's time we returned to the palace."

And bed? She assumed so as he led her to the palace in silence. Each step closer made her dread the night more, for though she longed to make love with him she knew she'd never win his heart.

At the door to her suite, he nudged her chin up and pressed an achingly tender kiss on her lips that brought tears to her eyes. "Get some rest, Demetria. The next few days will be hectic."

Then he turned and walked away. She stood there a moment, torn between letting him go and calling out to him, calling him back to her arms, to her bed.

She choked back a sob. Swiped trembling hands over her now wet cheeks, and stepped inside her lonely suite.

Love shouldn't hurt like this.

Demetria didn't see Kristo at all the next week. The following Saturday, the day that was to have been their wedding, was the funeral for Prince Gregor.

Like everything else Greek, the ceremony was laden with ritual and seemed endless. Demetria, wearing a black cashmere Donna Karan sheath, sat beside Kristo, who was resplendent in a black suit, black shirt and tie, with the royal sash stretched across his broad chest.

He was regal and unapproachable.

By the time the service was over and Prince Gregor had been buried in the royal family plot, she was exhausted in body and spirit. Still, she was obliged to stay until the guests left. Until the palace grew quiet.

Kristo had disappeared again, likely dealing with more state business, more duty that required his immediate attention. Her father and her unusually sedate sister had also left, so she had nobody to talk to. No one to share her thoughts with.

But, considering how troubled they were, perhaps that was for the best too.

She sought out her room, to get a few moments' peace and quiet. But she found little serenity there either.

The palace gardens were still in a state of half-readiness for the wedding. Her ivory gown hung on the form out of the light, ready for her to step into it. But when would that be?

The Royal House of Stanrakis would be in mourning for thirty days. A month to grieve. To wait to marry.

She didn't look forward to biding her time in the palace, where she'd have absolutely nothing to do. She wouldn't have any official duties until she married. It would be the longest month of her life.

Her door opened and Kristo strode in—tall, handsome and still formidable. But at least he'd come to her. At least now they could have some private time together.

"I trust you don't mind that I returned here to my suite?" she said. "I would have told you myself, but I didn't know where you'd gone."

"I had pressing business to attend to."

"That's what I thought." Tension pulsed between them,

leaving her more unsettled than before. "Is something wrong?" The resolute expression planted on his handsome face filled her with alarm.

"I've given this much thought. There is no reason for you to stay in residence through the period of mourning."

She stared at him, unable to believe he was sending her away. "You want me to leave Angyra for a month?"

He loosed an impatient shrug. "This is a good time to reevaluate what we have here."

"What?"

"You said it yourself. You want to marry for love." He stalked to the French doors and stared out, his expression brooding. "Of course if you're with child we will proceed with the wedding."

"What about the betrothal contract?"

"As King, I can alter such things."

She dropped onto the nearest chair, knowing her shaky legs wouldn't support her another moment. "Are you saying you'll only marry me now if I'm pregnant?"

He faced her then, and she'd never seen him look so remote. His lips pulled into a thin, disagreeable line. His magnetic eyes were closed to all emotion.

"There will be no bastards in the Royal House of Stanrakis."

"Don't you mean there will be no *more* bastards, for you are certainly acting the part now," she lashed out, hurt that he really cared so little for her.

"Think what you will. Unless you carry my heir, we are free to walk away from each other now if we wish."

If we wish... Her eyes and the back of her throat burned, for leaving him was the last thing she wanted to do. And yet pride wouldn't let her plead her point.

He'd made his wishes clear. There was no love between

them, just passion that would one day fade. Perhaps it already had. He would marry her only to legitimize an heir.

"If you leave today, you will be able to attend the Athens show."

"Yes." But the excitement that had once kept her awake at nights failed to materialize.

Her partner would have finished the designs. All would be in order, ready for the show. All except her.

How ironic that she'd once thought of nothing but pursuing that dream. Now that Kristo was letting her go, her heart simply wasn't in it. Her heart belonged here, with Kristo. But telling him that would change nothing.

He didn't love her.

He'd never love her.

"My jet will be ready to depart when you wish," he said, again in a cold, dismissive manner. "You'll let me know if you're pregnant?"

"Yes," she hissed, knowing that he'd likely have her watched, that she'd not be able to hide a child from him.

All the passion they'd shared was for naught. He'd likely begun to tire of her already, and without love there was nothing to keep them together. Nothing but duty. And he was willing to release her from that unless she was carrying his heir.

Tears stung her eyes, but she refused to cry. She'd leave with her head high, pride intact. Heart shattered.

She lifted her chin and faked a calm she was far from feeling. "I'd like to leave within the hour."

He gave a curt nod, his face wiped clean of emotion. "I'll inform the pilot. Vasos will see you to the airport."

"Thank you." She bit her lip, thinking this was all too abrupt, too cruel.

He stared at her. His gaze dropped to her mouth, lingered, setting off that low heat inside her again. She was sure he'd take her in his arms. That he'd give her a kiss that would blaze hot in her memory for the next month.

She hoped he'd at least tell her he'd miss her.

But he did neither.

King Kristo turned on his heel and strode from the room.

And in the awful quiet that settled around her she stopped trying to hold back the flood of burning tears.

Kristo sat in the dark in the royal office, a glass of ouzo in his hand and a half-empty bottle on the desk. For two days he'd racked his brain over his decision.

He'd rehearsed how to tell her.

He'd expected shocked surprise. A bit of anger, even. But he hadn't thought she'd tremble like a leaf caught in the wind. Hadn't thought those big eyes would swim with tears and hurt.

Seeing that had nearly toppled his resolve.

For a tense moment he'd struggled to regain control, fought the urge to drag her into his arms and give them both what they wanted. Sex.

Ah, but that was the problem, not the solution.

She wanted love.

He wanted sex.

There was no middle ground. No way this could ever be resolved unless she settled for his terms of marriage.

And that realization was what had finally gotten through to him. If he forced her to marry him he'd ultimately crush her spirit. She'd come to resent him for what he'd taken from her. What he could never give her.

Yes, this separation would do them both good. She could delve into the work she longed to pursue, and he would systematically purge this unacceptable craving for her from his system.

He'd done the right thing by letting her go.

So why the hell did he feel as if he'd made the biggest mistake of his life?

CHAPTER TWELVE

Six weeks later, Demetria sat at the drafting table in her flat in Athens. The show had been a success—so much so that she'd been invited to participate in an exclusive exhibition in London next week.

But the creativity that had never failed her before had yet to resurrect itself. Nothing new had come to mind. Nothing even remotely innovative.

No, all her thoughts centered around Kristo. Over a month had passed and he'd yet to contact her. News out of Angyra had been ominously absent since Gregor's funeral.

Not so the paparazzi. They hounded her every move, robbing her of sleep and keeping her on edge. She'd become a prisoner in her own flat, for she couldn't keep ignoring their questions. Had Kristo set a new date for the wedding? Had she spoken with him? Was the wedding off? Whose decision had it been to cancel it? Had Kristo tired of her? Had she jilted the King of Angyra for her career as a designer?

On and on the questions would go, until she wanted to crawl in a hole and hide forever. Which was pretty much what she'd done. Stayed in her flat and moped.

"You can't go on like this," her partner Yannis said, his thin face showing grave concern. "Phone him."

Her fingers tightened around her pencil, her insides clenching with the misery that just wouldn't let go. "I did yesterday morning, but the line was busy."

Always busy. For the same thing had happened the day before. And the day before that.

She refused to leave a message informing Kristo that she was pregnant. That she was carrying the royal baby in her womb. That he'd be obliged to marry her now.

So she'd abruptly hung up—for what else could she say except that she was miserable? That she missed him dreadfully?

Pride wouldn't let her do that.

"I was thinking that your name should be on our label instead of mine," she said.

"Changing the subject will not make it go away," said Yannis.

Damn him for being right, for knowing her so well. "I'm serious. I feel guilty that you didn't get the credit you deserved at the show."

He spread his arms wide. "My time will come."

"Soon, I would wager."

She glanced at the new garments he'd designed, in awe of his originality.

Now was her chance to shine. What she'd always wanted was in her grasp. But all she could think of was Kristo. Of their baby. Of the loveless future that awaited them.

Could her heart break any more than it already had? Could she possibly get more despondent?

Yannis was right. It was time to get on with her life. She had a baby to think of, to raise. To love.

Kristo's baby.

Time was supposedly the great healer, but her heart ached when she thought of losing Kristo. If she closed her eyes she could almost feel his hands and mouth on her, hear his heart beating in tandem with hers.

"Enough is enough. You need a diversion, and the upcoming exhibition in London will be ideal," Yannis said.

She was shaking her head before he'd finished. "I'm not up to being thrust in the limelight."

He jabbed a thumb at the window. "You're happy to stay here like a prisoner, with the paparazzi camped outside your door? Hoping he'll call?"

"No! But attending the exhibition means I'll have to face publicity head-on, and I'm not ready for that." Not nearly strong enough to field questions about her relationship with one arrogant King.

"The sponsors will have security, so you won't be hounded." Yannis knelt before her and took her cold hands in his. "Demetria, come to London. You need to get away."

She took a breath. Nodded. "All right."

Kristo paused at the rear of the large hall and gave a dismissive glance at the rail-thin models gliding down the catwalk under the swaths of strobe lights. The crush of the audience was as displeasing as the accompanying music that throbbed in the auditorium.

The only thing more distasteful than this chaos was the swarm of paparazzi clustered outside on the Strand. But these same gossipmongers in London were the ones who'd advertised the fact that Demetria had been specially invited to present her creations at this elite show for five new designers.

A phone call to the promoter of the event—a gentleman who was a fellow conservationist as well as a shrewd gambler—had secured him backstage passage. But he was painfully aware that wouldn't guarantee Demetria being pleased to see him.

So be it. He'd suffered six long weeks of misery without her, though he'd been slow to realize why. How strange that it had taken a bottle of Lesvos ouzo and an aged royal gardener to clear the fog from his mind.

"Your Majesty," a stout man said as he hurried toward him, his worried gaze flicking from Vasos to Kristo. "Please, if you'll come this way I'll show you backstage. Unless of course you wish to watch the remainder of the show here?"

"Backstage is fine."

"Very well." The man set a fast pace down the corridor and he followed, with Vasos trailing him.

He had no desire to be a part of the audience—especially when every nerve in his body had gone tight at the promise of seeing Demetria again. Why the hell had he let her go?

Pride. He wouldn't delve into the new feelings tormenting him. Guilt over the way he'd treated her—for she wasn't a chattel to be handed from one lord to the other: she was a beautiful, desirable woman. *Innocent* woman. Stupidity for thinking for one moment that he could live without her.

He couldn't.

Angyra couldn't.

They expected a royal wedding any day. They expected the bride to be Demetria, the woman they adored.

He adored.

If he hadn't been so stubbornly blind he'd have realized that six weeks ago. No, longer ago than that.

Over a year ago, when they'd first met on the beach. He'd known then down deep that she was unlike any woman he'd ever met before. Known she was perfect for him.

But again he'd let pride and jealousy blind him. He should have gone to Gregor immediately. He should have seen the truth in her innocence and fought for her hand then.

Ah, he had made so many mistakes with her. Would she grant him absolution now? Or would he forever be thrust into this personal hell of wanting her from afar?

The questions and doubts hammered away at him as the

man led them past the guards into the dimly lit backstage area. The spacious area was crowded like the Grand Bazaar in Istanbul, with sections partitioned off with stark white sheets.

He followed the man through the labyrinth. Past the impromptu studios that teemed with frantic designers and models in all stages of dress to the last tented room.

The letter *delta* was painted on the billowing sheet that served as a door. *D* for Demetria?

"This is her staging area, Your Majesty." The man managed a clumsy bow and disappeared.

Kristo pushed the curtain aside and stepped into her domain. Impatience pounded in his veins as he looked beyond the crush of models and artisans who made up the design team for a sign of Demetria. But all he saw were strangers.

The sharp clap of hands brought everyone's head up. "Ten minutes, ladies. Let's be ready. Ari! Do something about the neckline on this dress," a man barked, and then moved on to the next model, who stood there in a scrap of a bra and panties, waiting to be dressed like a child.

Kristo narrowed his eyes on the man issuing orders. If anyone knew where she was, it would be this abrupt man.

He crossed to the man in an economy of movement. "Where is Demetria?"

The man's head snapped up, light brown eyes flashing with annoyance. Then came the slightest widening of his eyes before they snapped back to match his scowl.

"So you choose now to finally show up?" the man said, foregoing any respect for the crown and Kristo was sure for himself as well.

He muttered a curse. "Why I am here is none of your business."

"On the contrary. I'm Demi's partner and her friend," the

man said. "You ruined her debut in Athens. Now, stay out of sight and out of the way and let her have this moment."

The truth was the slap in the face that he deserved, for he hadn't let her go until the very eve of the Athens show. She couldn't possibly have been prepared for it.

He gave a curt nod and moved behind a screen to stand and watch and wait when he longed to find Demetria. To hold her. Kiss her. Make love to her.

His heart gave an odd thud the second he saw her hurry toward a model draped in a muted floral gown. Seeing her again was a punch to his gut, bringing back memories that had never left him, reminding him of days at the palace. Of nights in her arms.

She moved away from the throng of models and he immediately noted the changes in her. She'd lost weight, and there were obvious lines of stress marring her beautiful face.

He ached to go to her, to take her in his arms, to take her away from here. Back to Angyra. To the palace and his bed. He wanted her so badly he could savor the satin of her skin against his lips, feel the comfort of her arms around him, the rightness of her body as he sank into her.

He wanted her more than he ever had before. Wanted her now. But her partner was right. This was *her* moment, not his.

She gave the model's abbreviated skirt a final adjustment and smiled. "Walk down the runway like you own the world."

As soon as the girl did as she was bid, Demetria turned back to the next model in line. Only the person behind her was him.

She went still, and stared at him a long moment, the air around them charged with desire, need and another emotion he had just recently come to grips with.

It still scared him to admit how he felt, for it made him

look at the man he'd been in a whole new light. He hadn't liked what he'd seen. Hadn't liked the man he'd become. Domineering. Aloof. Alone.

He was like Angyra—adrift in the sea.

His mother had told him to marry for love. His brother had simply said a man should love his wife.

Love. What did they know that he didn't? Why was this emotion so difficult for him to understand?

Now he knew. Now he hoped to hell he wasn't too late.

She stepped toward him and stopped, staring hard, as if trying to decide if he were real or imagined. "Kristo?"

He allowed a brief smile as his hungry gaze swept over her thin form again. There was nothing to indicate she was with child. Nothing binding them now. Nothing that would make this easy.

His jaw clenched. He didn't deserve easy. He needed to put effort into this—as much as with any deal he'd ever made or more. For his future hinged on this moment. On her.

Yet even now that would have to wait. People were watching them. Listening.

He noted Yannis was looking for her, looking frantic when he spotted them together. "Go on with what you are doing," Kristo said. "I'll wait here until the show is over."

He would wait forever for her if he must.

She hesitated a long moment, as if unsure what to do, as if not trusting he'd stay. But then what had he ever done to instill trust in her?

"Demi," her partner said. "They want you onstage."

"Coming." She turned and hurried back to the designer and the nervous models clustered just offstage, back to her world.

Kristo listened to Demetria's credentials and the short list of her styles presented today. Applause rang in the hall. Her partner motioned her to take the stage, but she balked.

"We both know this is your show," she said to Yannis, surprising Kristo, who'd inched forward to watch, to admire her in action. In control. "If not for you and Ari I wouldn't have been invited to this showing."

"We just held things together until you returned," Yannis said, and all but pushed her out on the stage. "Go. Accept the honor and praise you deserve."

Kristo bunched his hands at his sides as she took hesitant steps out onto the stage. She looked so small out there. So alone. So removed from him.

I could lose her right now. Forever.

That possibility clutched at his heart, paining him as nothing else had. Losing her would devastate him. Leave a scar that would never heal.

"Thank you for your enthusiastic applause," Demetria said to the crowd, her voice surprisingly strong. "But much of the credit goes to my partner, Yannis Petropoulos."

The audience clapped, but before the applause had fully died down, before she'd exited the stage, a man called out, "Miss Andreou? Will you give up designing if you marry the King of Angyra?"

"Is the wedding still on?" another shouted.

An immediate hush fell over the hall, followed by a ripple of nervous whispers. Instead of answering, Demetria simply waved and returned backstage.

It was then that he noticed the tears glistening in her eyes. She stopped to exchange one fierce hug with her partner, but her gaze remained on Kristo.

His heart started thundering as she pulled away and walked toward him. She stopped just out of arm's reach, eyes now dry but wary. "Why did you come?"

Because he couldn't sleep, couldn't eat for wanting her. Because without her his life simply wasn't the same.

But he wasn't about to tell her that here—not with so many

eyes watching them. "That should be obvious," he said, and when she frowned, he huffed out a sigh. "Please. I have a limo waiting outside. We can talk there in private."

Her solemn eyes, with dark lashes still spiked with moisture, searched Kristo's face—questioning. Sad.

He wondered about her thoughts. Wondered if she'd refuse. Wondered if anything or anyone could drag her away from this exciting world.

"This sounds serious," she said, her voice barely above a whisper.

He couldn't begin to tell her how much. How he was barely able to draw a breath for fear that she'd refuse him.

"Extremely so." He extended his hand to her, when he longed to sweep her into his arms and storm out of here.

Her luminous gaze flicked from his palm to his face. The slender column of her throat worked. Then to his relief the hesitation in her eyes slowly ebbed away.

"Very well. I'll go with you."

Slowly, hesitantly, she placed her hand in his. And for the first time in hours he was able to breathe.

"Are you happy, *agapi mou*?"

She was miserable, moody, weepy. Heartsick from wanting him. From longing for the love he'd denied her.

"It's been trying, with the paparazzi watching my every move," she said instead, still desperately clinging to what remained of her pride.

"The world waits to see what you will create. You are an up-and-coming high fashion designer," he said. "You will dazzle the world."

Exactly what she'd dreamed of doing for years. Yet now that the possibility of success loomed on her horizon she'd lost the passion to pour her heart and soul into her art.

All because she'd been swept up in the turmoil that

surrounded this demanding man. Because the weeks since leaving Angyra had been utter hell. Because the royal heir was nestled in her womb, and that sealed her fate.

"What is troubling you, *agapi mou*?" he asked, grasping her hand and entwining their fingers.

The strong, steady pulse of him vibrated into her, drawing her into him, muddling her senses. She took a breath, then another, yet still felt as if her world was about to spin out of control.

Tell him! Spit it out and end this torture!

"You," she said. "I don't know whether to be happy to see you again, or to dread the outcome of this visit."

Silence throbbed between them as she waited for him to say something correct. Something that would put an end to this turmoil, this hoping that he'd come for her.

He huffed out a rough sigh. "We are our own worst enemies. Always at odds. Hesitant to trust."

Her throat was thick with tears and her eyes burned. Sitting beside him, holding his hand and feeling that strong sensual pull ribbon around her, was tearing her apart inside.

"When you sent me away, you hurt me more than I ever thought possible," she admitted, and felt him go deathly still beside her. "But I never stopped loving you. I couldn't even when I tried. And now that I'm…I'm…"

"Shh," he soothed, pulling her into his arms, where she'd ached to be for so long. "I'm a bastard for putting you through this emotional hell when all you asked for was my heart. Do you know why I couldn't give that to you, *agapi mou*?"

She shook her head on a choked sob, afraid to guess why.

"Because I didn't know what love was. Because I'd forgotten the wisdom passed down to me from a wise old man."

"The King?" she guessed.

"No. Someone far wiser than my austere father," he said.

"When I was six years old I saw our old gardener on the cliff path with his wife, walking hand in hand. I'd never seen a man and woman do that before, and I asked him why they did it. He told me that he'd given his heart to her when he was a young man and that their love had never dimmed for one day."

"How beautiful," she said, blinking back the sting of tears, envious of the old couple and yet deeply touched that such love existed.

The oddest smile curved Kristo's sensuous mouth. "I never saw my parents touch each other, though it is obvious my mother did her duty and gave my father three sons. But there was no tenderness between them. No passion." His hand tightened on hers. Warm. Strong. "No holding hands."

She thought back to her own childhood and sighed. "There was no hand-holding between my father and stepmother either, though there were many bouts of raised voices and arguments."

She'd hated the turmoil. Hated the constant upheaval in their lives that had kept her and her sister cowering.

He cleared his throat and stroked her thumb with his. "I vowed then that if I ever married it would be to a woman who'd captured my heart. When I first met you on the beach I was instantly attracted to you. I wanted you more than I'd ever wanted a woman, and those stolen kisses and caresses only left me wanting you more," he said.

"Until you discovered who I was," she said, her voice small.

"Exactly. I hated my brother for being the man to have won you. I hated you for allowing me such liberties."

Heat burned her cheeks, but a new warmth stirred in her at his admission. If only it hadn't been lust that drew them together...

She gave a shuddering sigh. "I hated myself for betraying

Gregor, but I, too, was powerless to walk away from you. But you know that already."

And it had made no difference to how he felt about her. She'd always be the woman who had betrayed the Crown Prince.

"It is time we move forward with our lives," he said, and she felt her breath seize, fearing the farewell that was sure to come.

She couldn't let him voice that final goodbye—not before she told him about their love-child. "We can't—"

"You will let me finish," he said, and pressed two fingers against her lips. But it was the fierce look in his eyes that silenced her.

"I have done many things wrong with you," he said. "But this time it will be done right. I love you, *agapi mou*."

She blinked, stunned to hear the words she'd feared he'd never voice.

Was she dreaming? "You do?"

He gathered her close and kissed her so tenderly that tears spilled down her cheeks. "Will you forgive me for being an arrogant fool? Will you marry me? Will you be the woman I give my heart to, who'll walk in the garden with me hand in hand when we are both old?"

"Yes." She lifted her face to his, gazing into dark eyes that showed the depth of his love, that proved to her this was not a dream.

This was real. And this was right.

"Yes," she said, this time from her heart. "I'll love you now, when we are old, with my last breath and through eternity."

"To the airport," he told his driver, his voice gruff with emotion. "To Angyra and our future."

She took his right hand and placed it over her still-flat stomach. "To our baby."

His dark eyes flickered with surprise. With joy. "You're pregnant?"

"Yes," she said. "I tried to tell you earlier, but you kept interrupting me."

He flashed her a smile that was deliciously wicked. "Which is what I am going to do again, now that you have made me the happiest man on earth."

Then he pulled her close to his heart, as if she were his most valued treasure, and kissed her deeply, leaving no doubt that their love would last a lifetime and beyond.

* * * * *

Coming Next Month

from **Harlequin Presents® EXTRA.** Available December 7, 2010.

#129 HIS CHRISTMAS VIRGIN
Carole Mortimer
Christmas Surrender

#130 SNOWBOUND SEDUCTION
Helen Brooks
Christmas Surrender

#131 RED WINE AND HER SEXY EX
Kate Hardy
Unfinished Business

#132 CAUGHT ON CAMERA WITH THE CEO
Natalie Anderson
Unfinished Business

Coming Next Month

from **Harlequin Presents®.** Available December 28, 2010.

#2963 THE RELUCTANT SURRENDER
Penny Jordan
The Parenti Dynasty

#2964 ANNIE AND THE RED-HOT ITALIAN
Carole Mortimer
The Balfour Brides

#2965 THE BRIDE THIEF
Jennie Lucas

#2966 THE LAST KOLOVSKY PLAYBOY
Carol Marinelli

#2967 THE SOCIETY WIFE
India Grey
Bride on Approval

#2968 RECKLESS IN PARADISE
Trish Morey

REQUEST YOUR FREE BOOKS!

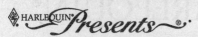

2 FREE NOVELS PLUS
2 FREE GIFTS!

YES! Please send me 2 FREE Harlequin Presents® novels and my 2 FREE gifts (gifts are worth about $10). After receiving them, if I don't wish to receive any more books, I can return the shipping statement marked "cancel." If I don't cancel, I will receive 6 brand-new novels every month and be billed just $4.05 per book in the U.S. or $4.74 per book in Canada. That's a saving of at least 15% off the cover price! It's quite a bargain! Shipping and handling is just 50¢ per book.* I understand that accepting the 2 free books and gifts places me under no obligation to buy anything. I can always return a shipment and cancel at any time. Even if I never buy another book, the two free books and gifts are mine to keep forever.

106/306 HDN E5M4

Name	(PLEASE PRINT)	
Address		Apt. #
City	State/Prov.	Zip/Postal Code

Signature (if under 18, a parent or guardian must sign)

Mail to the **Harlequin Reader Service**:
IN U.S.A.: P.O. Box 1867, Buffalo, NY 14240-1867
IN CANADA: P.O. Box 609, Fort Erie, Ontario L2A 5X3

Not valid for current subscribers to Harlequin Presents books.

Are you a current subscriber to Harlequin Presents books and want to receive the larger-print edition? Call 1-800-873-8635 today!

* Terms and prices subject to change without notice. Prices do not include applicable taxes. N.Y. residents add applicable sales tax. Canadian residents will be charged applicable provincial taxes and GST. Offer not valid in Quebec. This offer is limited to one order per household. All orders subject to approval. Credit or debit balances in a customer's account(s) may be offset by any other outstanding balance owed by or to the customer. Please allow 4 to 6 weeks for delivery. Offer available while quantities last.

Your Privacy: Harlequin Books is committed to protecting your privacy. Our Privacy Policy is available online at www.eHarlequin.com or upon request from the Reader Service. From time to time we make our lists of customers available to reputable third parties who may have a product or service of interest to you. If you would prefer we not share your name and address, please check here. ☐

Help us get it right—We strive for accurate, respectful and relevant communications. To clarify or modify your communication preferences, visit us at www.ReaderService.com/consumerchoice.

HP10R

HARLEQUIN®

A Romance

FOR EVERY MOOD™

Spotlight on

Classic

Quintessential, modern love stories
that are romance at its finest.

See the next page
to enjoy a sneak peek from
the Harlequin Presents® series.

*Harlequin Presents® is thrilled
to introduce the first installment of
an epic tale of passion and drama by*
USA TODAY *Bestselling Author*
Penny Jordan!

*When buttoned-up Giselle first meets
the devastatingly handsome Saul Parenti,
the heat between them is explosive....*

"LET ME GET THIS STRAIGHT. Are you actually suggesting that I would stoop to that kind of game playing?"

Saul came out from behind his desk and walked toward her. Giselle could smell his hot male scent and it was making her dizzy, igniting a low, dull, pulsing ache that was taking over her whole body.

Giselle defended her suspicions. "You don't want me here."

"No," Saul agreed, "I don't."

And then he did what he had sworn he would not do, cursing himself beneath his breath as he reached for her, pulling her fiercely into his arms and kissing her with all the pent-up fury she had aroused in him from the moment he had first seen her.

Giselle certainly *wanted* to resist him. But the hand she raised to push him away developed a will of its own and was sliding along his bare arm beneath the sleeve of his shirt, and the body that should have been arching away from him was instead melting into him.

Beneath the pressure of his kiss he could feel and taste her gasp of undeniable response to him. He wanted to devour her, take her and drive them both until they were equally satiated—even whilst the anger within him that she should make him feel that way roared and burned its resentment of his need.

She was helpless, Giselle recognized, totally unable to withstand the storm lashing at her, able only to cling to the man who was the cause of it and pray that she would survive.

Somewhere else in the building a door banged. The sound exploded into the sensual tension that had enclosed them, driving them apart. Saul's chest was rising and falling as he fought for control; Giselle's whole body was trembling.

Without a word she turned and ran.

Find out what happens when Saul and Giselle succumb to their irresistible desire in

THE RELUCTANT SURRENDER

Available January 2011 from Harlequin Presents®

HARLEQUIN® *Romance*®

MARGARET WAY

Wealthy Australian, Secret Son

Rohan was Charlotte's shining white knight
until he disappeared—before she had
the chance to tell him she was pregnant.

But when Rohan returns years later as
a self-made millionaire, could the blond,
blue-eyed little boy and Charlotte's heart
keep him from leaving again?

Available January 2011

HRI7704